~1203
~604

DATE DUE

OCT 02

JE 05 '03			
JY 10 '03			
AG 19 '03			
FEB 18 2014			
OCT 20 2014			
MAR 16			
GAYLORD			PRINTED IN U.S.A.

THAT
Champagne
Feeling

**Center Point
Large Print**

**This Large Print Book carries the
Seal of Approval of N.A.V.H.**

ॐ श्री गणेशाय नमः

Jane Feather

WRITING AS
CLAUDIA BISHOP

THAT Champagne Feeling

Center Point Publishing
Thorndike, Maine

This Center Point Large Print edition
is published in the year 2002 by arrangement with
The Berkley Publishing Group, a division of Penguin Putnam Inc.

The text of this Large Print edition is unabridged. In other
aspects, this book may vary from the original edition. Printed in
Thailand. Set in 16-point Times New Roman type by
Bill Coskrey and Gary Socquet.

ISBN 1-58547-229-8

Cataloging-in-Publication data is available from the Library of Congress.

1

"*WHERE* ARE WE GOING?" Emma settled herself on the seat of the cab and turned determinedly toward her husband of a few hours as he pulled the door shut behind him and almost in the same movement drew her tightly into the circle of his arm.

"The Copley Plaza," Mark replied promptly.

"For three whole weeks?" Emma asked, snuggling contentedly against his chest.

"No, Emma mine. For just long enough for me to discover the secret of that gorgeous, sexy dress of yours." He laughed softly, bending to cover her mouth with his.

"And what then?" she whispered, her body beginning to glow as his hand slid beneath her cape to the soft, full swell of her breasts, molding them in his palm.

"Why, then, my darling, we are going to play for a very, very long time." The tip of his tongue flicked the lobe of her ear in that special way he had.

Emma shivered deliciously. "How long?"

"A lifetime."

"I think, my love, that you are a white slaver masquerading as a psychiatrist," Emma told him playfully. "You're going to whisk me off to some Arabian harem and sell me to the highest bidder! Why else would you be so secretive?"

"I've already told you." Mark smiled and ran his long fingers over her eyelids, along the bridge of her nose. "For the next three weeks, we are going to forget about work totally. I'm taking you on a mystery voyage to never-never land, sweet, and you are going to forget all about the hospital, the kids' unit, and every professional facet of Emma Grantham. For the duration of our honeymoon, I want to eat, sleep, and above all *love* with Mrs. Forrest—all right?"

"You won't share your bed with Dr. Grantham?"

"Absolutely not!"

"I'll tell her to go home, then," Emma murmured contentedly, snuggling against him.

A slight, apologetic cough from the driver's seat brought them both hastily upright. It was a fairly short drive from Emma's house, where the marriage ceremony and reception had taken place, to the Copley Plaza, and she felt an absurd urge to giggle as Mark, straight-faced, felt for his wallet and the doorman ceremoniously ushered her out of the cab. Mark's arm circled her shoulder possessively as they entered the elegant lobby of the hotel.

"Suite four-oh-two, Dr. Forrest, Mrs. Forrest," the desk clerk said, handing the bellman a key. Emma hid a grin. This was going to take some getting used to. They had agreed she would keep her own name, but clearly there were going to be some occasions when insisting on it would be rather silly; a honeymoon was one of those occasions.

Their suite was everything the Copley Plaza had promised—quiet, old-fashioned, elegant, and comfortable; a throwback to the Boston of the old days, which was a far cry from the anonymous homogeneity of a Hilton or a Sheraton.

As Mark tipped the bellman, Emma went to the window and looked out over the lighted city as it began the New Year. She had been born and raised in Boston, and despite the years she had lived in New York while attending medical school there and as many excursions to Europe as an impoverished medical student could manage, she was a New Englander to her bones, and Boston was the hub of civilization for her. And so, when the opportunity to do her psychiatric internship at St. Anne's, a large private non-profit psychiatric hospital, had come up, she had seized it eagerly. This was her hometown where she had spent a near-perfect childhood, and she could now use her expertise to repay the city for some of that pleasure. Both her parents had been doctors, and the Boston medical world was utterly familiar territory that she had slipped into as easily as an old pair of comfortable shoes.

When Emma had passed her boards and gotten her license as a psychiatrist three years ago, her only sorrow had been that her parents were no longer alive to celebrate with her. But she had assuaged her grief with work, plunging herself into the tricky business of administration politics as she set about selling her concept of an innovative children's unit for St. Anne's to the hospital trustees and state officials. The method of treatment—emphasizing early diagnosis and prevention—was very expensive, and since Emma had insisted that the unit be available to all children in need of its services and not just to those of well-insured parents, it depended to a large extent on state funding.

It had been a hard grant to write convincingly for the dollar-minded hospital trustees and the state bureaucrats, and Emma had had to promise a degree of success that at times seemed almost impossible to maintain. But the kids' unit had, from its inception, been a model program, and for the last three years Emma's annual budget had been approved without argument. Yet Emma was no starry-eyed idealist; she knew that if the unit ever slipped a notch in its reputation and importance, the state would cut off the funds without remorse. She hated leaving the unit for a minute; when she was at the helm, it didn't matter too much that she and her staff habitually broke every bureaucratic rule in the book in the interests of good treatment. She knew what she was doing and why, and was fully prepared to defend her actions, but God only knew what could happen in the three weeks she was to be gone!

Mark sometimes worked with her in the unit and as a consultant. He understood her practices and principles and supported them wholeheartedly, but he was not a member of the regular staff, and the final responsibility was not his. He was the best child psychiatrist Emma had ever known, and his professional help was vital to the success of the program and to her own well-being, but he didn't have to fight the administration over every petty detail, and he wasn't ultimately responsible for the unit . . .

Mark closed the door firmly and turned to watch the still figure at the window, a slight smile curving his lips. Emma's dress was really something! The tawny gold velvet covered her from her throat to her ankles, and yet gave the distinct impression that she was wearing nothing underneath.

Clothes were Emma's one small vanity and her only large expense, he reflected. It was no wonder that Jacqueline, the mastermind behind the success of that chic boutique in Cambridge, was such a good friend of hers!

His mind drifted back to the first time he'd seen Emma

two and a half years ago, when, as a newly hired consultant, he had first walked onto the kids' unit at St. Anne's. Emma had been sitting on the floor of the dayroom, cuddling a very grubby, wet-nosed, tearstained little girl, totally heedless of the dirty fingerprints tracking down the front of her immaculate ivory silk shirt and over her beautifully creased white linen pants. She had raised her small, well-shaped head with its austere crown of cornsilk braids, and when those myopic, impossibly violet eyes smiled at him, he had been totally lost.

Not that she had been an easy conquest, he thought, grinning to himself reminiscently. She had been recovering from a divorce—an amicable one certainly, but nonetheless traumatic, particularly since it had left Emma to raise an eight-month-old baby alone. But then his Emma was an optimist. The cookie jar was always half full as far as she was concerned, and there was a solution to every problem. She didn't waste time and energy on self-pity. Anyone less self-pitying and more independent than his new bride would be hard to find. Not that Emma's spirited temperament and. maverick ways didn't cause a few sparks now and then, but Mark had always preferred spice to sugar, and from the start, he had known Emma was the one woman for him.

It had seemed an eternity before she finally capitulated to his determined but gentle pursuit. However, the capitulation had made the eternity well worthwhile! Right now, though, he could tell by the slight tension between her shoulder blades that her mind was not where he wished it to be. A little husbandly assertion seemed in order.

"Mrs. Forrest?" The quiet voice brought her whirling

guiltily to face him. "I thought Dr. Grantham had gone home?"

How was it that he always knew? Emma smiled in soft apology. "She has. It was just a momentary lapse."

"Not to be repeated, I hope." He took one wrist and carefully undid the tiny buttons on the sleeve before moving to the other one. Emma stood quietly in front of him, all thoughts of St. Anne's banished as she waited in breathless suspense for what was to come.

"I want you so much, my own." His voice rasped, husky with passion as he held her hands, looking deep into her eyes. "Let me possess you totally—just for tonight."

She freed her hands from the light grasp, raised her arms, and slipped them around his neck. "I'm all yours, my love, for this night and every night. Tell me what you want."

"You, Emma mine," he murmured, tipping her chin up as his lips found her throat. "You, to be for me alone."

A slow melting began as her knees became butter, as liquid sunshine spread through every muscle and joint, as she sank slowly against the firmness of his length. She felt her dress move slowly upward to her thighs under his deft hands, his expert fingers slipped inside the waist band of her pantyhose and pushed the delicate nylon gently off her hips, his soft chuckle rustling against her skin as he realized she was wearing nothing beneath them. He dropped to his knees, easing her feet into nakedness, before sliding his hands again up and under the tawny velvet skirt.

Emma inhaled sharply, biting her bottom lip as the music swelled within. Her legs parted involuntarily as he wordlessly raised her skirt, held it high against her buttocks while his mouth found the tender, opened bud of her passion. Then he took her away from reality into the farthest reaches of joyous infinity, and she gave him herself.

"Lord, you're so beautiful." Slowly, Mark rose to his feet, letting her skirt fall back in soft, sensuous folds against her skin. He held her face as his lips burned hers and she tasted of herself and her fulfillment.

"Turn around, sweet." He murmured the demand against her mouth. "I must have all of you."

"And I all of you," she murmured back, turning under his hands.

"Later, sweet, please. Give to me, now."

How could she ever want to do anything else? Emma stood still beneath the swift fingers unbuttoning the neck of her dress, pulling down the long, concealed zipper. The dress fell to her ankles; she stood naked in a sea of golden velvet.

"Why is it," he whispered against the soft, exposed nape of her neck, "that every time I see you, it's for the first time?"

A shiver ran through her; every nerve of her skin seemed to have surfaced, begging for the stimulation of those gentle, stroking hands. She leaned backward slightly, pressing her bare back against the texture of his clothing as his hands cradled the firm roundness of her buttocks, slid slowly around to caress her belly. A fingertip played delicately in the tight cup of her navel before his hands moved upward over the delineated rib cage to touch, with strong but gentle finger strokes, the longing swell of her breasts.

It was so very hard to keep still when she wanted so much to hold him, strip him of his clothes, caress and devour his body with her hands and mouth. But he wanted her passivity tonight, and she held herself back, desire and excitement mounting to an almost unmanageable fever. He was unpinning the neat coronet of her hair, letting the long, tight braids fall down her back.

"Sit," he whispered urgently, pushing her toward the dresser stool in front of the long mirror. She complied silently, her body gleaming white and vulnerable against the dark gray of his suit. He freed the cornsilk hair of all restraint as his fingers worked through the strands, loosening the waves. Then he flipped open a suitcase and reached for a hairbrush, beginning with long, rhythmic strokes to smooth the shining mane as it fell to her shoulder blades. Her head bent as he stroked her scalp, brushing the full length of her hair; the bristles of the brush prickled the skin of her neck, her back, until the long, straight river of sunshine glistened under the lamplight.

Mark parted the tresses at her back and tossed them over her shoulders, where they hung covering her breasts. His long fingers reached over to separate the strands, to reveal the closed, pink buds peeping through their silken covering.

Emma watched her image in the mirror in bemused fascination, as she saw the creamy mounds of her breasts, startlingly blue-veined, so slowly exposed. Her eyes met Mark's in the glass, and they became lost in each other's image as their reflections melded under the hooded intensity of desire. His hands were at her waist now, drawing her to her feet with quiet, controlled insistence; her hands fluttered toward his tie, the buttons of his shirt, but Mark shook his head gently as he guided her backward to the bed. The edge caught her behind the knees and she subsided easily onto the mattress, looking up at him, her love, her husband, as those warm brown eyes swept her body with a posses-sive tenderness that filled her with joy.

"Oh, Emma mine!" Mark dropped to the bed and sat astride her, kneading her shoulders, caressing her arms, tracing her breasts with feathery fingers. "You are mine, my love. Tell me you are."

"All yours, my darling. Do with me as you wish." They had laughed and loved before, played together gloriously, but never before had he asked this of her, that she offer her womanhood and demand nothing. But there was no need to demand—by giving in this way, she would receive. Mark was enjoying her, and his enjoyment was her own.

He played with her, turning and twisting her body under hands and tongue, and she crested wave after wondrous wave before, finally, he stood to remove his clothes and she was able to reach for him, to feel the long hardness of him as, at long last, he entered her. It was as if they had never made love before, as if it were happening for the first time, but with the paradoxical familiarity of established lovers who knew how to please each other.

The wintry dawn of the New Year was breaking as they rolled off the bed, staggered toward the shower, with sleepy, exhausted, loving hands washed each other, dived between the rumpled sheets, pulled up the chaotically dis-arranged covers, curled tightly, warm body against warm body, and fell into a deep, languorous sleep.

Emma awoke to a darkened room lit by the soft glow of the bedside lamp and lay for a moment in bewildered relax-ation as she struggled to orient herself. Turning her head on the pillow, she looked toward the window. It wasn't exactly dark outside, but there was a lowering, snow-threatening gloom. Mark was standing naked, looking out, one hand absently drying his neck with a towel. Drops of water glistened on the long, rippling back, and his normally wavy dark brown hair had, as usual after a shower, sprung into tight curls. She smiled, drinking him with her eyes, reveling in the joy of watching him like this as he stood, deep in thought, unaware of her scrutiny.

"You have such a cute bottom." She broke the silence softly.

He turned and with a quiet laugh came across to the bed. "Good afternoon, madam wife."

"It's not, is it?" She struggled onto one elbow, reaching for her watch.

"Three o'clock." He chuckled.

"But that means we've slept all day!"

"Well, since we didn't sleep all night, that seems entirely reasonable." He grinned mischievously. "How are you?"

She stretched languidly beneath the sheet, running remembering hands over her warm body. "Wonderful," she sighed, "but just the tiniest bit sore."

"Hardly surprising!" He bent to kiss the corner of her mouth.

"Do I look as debauched as I feel?" she teased.

"Let's see." He took her face between his hands, examining her with mock gravity. "I think that rather depends on just how debauched you feel."

"Utterly!" she replied promptly.

He laughed, kissed her again, "You look very well loved, my precious, as well loved as I hope you know you are."

Emma nodded with quiet satisfaction, wrapping her arms

around his neck. A knock at the door ended the beginnings of what promised to become a rather long session.

"That, I hope, is our breakfast." Mark stood up, and strode toward the door.

"Mark!" she exclaimed with a whoop of laughter. "You can't open the door like that!"

"Oh, Lord! I must be losing my mind!" He pulled the damp towel from his neck and wrapped it swiftly around his waist. Emma buried her head under the covers as gales of hilarity swept through her. She remained hidden, a heaving mound beneath the sheet, until the door shut behind the room-service waiter.

"Come out of there, you ridiculous creature!" Mark pulled the sheet back, his eyes dancing with merriment. "Have you the faintest idea how embarrassing that was? It's three o'clock in the afternoon, I'm wearing nothing but a skimpy towel that does little to hide my . . . er . . . stimulated condition, and the bed's shaking as if there were an earthquake. The poor man didn't know where to look!"

Still convulsed, Emma wiped her streaming eyes on the sheet. "He must be used to honeymoon couples by now, surely!"

"Let's hope so," Mark responded dryly, and turned toward the room-service cart with its silver-covered dishes, heavy cutlery, and snowy linen. "Come eat now."

She hopped out of bed, came to the table, lifted the lid on a dish. "Oysters Rockefeller for breakfast!"

"It's a compromise." Grinning, he lifted a bottle of champagne out of an ice bucket. "It *is* the middle of the afternoon, after all. But in deference to our newly awakened state, we will commit sacrilege and dilute the Veuve Clicquot with orange juice." The cork exploded resoundingly, and the golden liquid foamed over his hands as he swiftly reached for the glasses.

"I think," Emma stated firmly, taking a long sip of her freshly squeezed orange juice and champagne, "that I could become used to starting the day like this."

"If you're going to sit opposite me in nothing but your skin," Mark muttered plaintively, "we'll never start the day at all!"

Emma merely smiled sweetly and continued with her breakfast.

Half an hour later, there was nothing left on the table. "I didn't realize how hungry I was," she declared, wiping her mouth vigorously before stretching with the deep satisfaction of repletion.

Mark groaned as her breasts lifted with the movement, the skin drawn taut against her ribs. "If you don't hit the shower and get some clothes on, Emma mine, we're going to miss our plane," he said carefully.

Emma straightened suddenly. "*Where* are we going?" This time she was determined to get an answer.

"Wait and see." He grinned.

"No, Mark Forrest, I will *not* wait for one more minute." Rising, she walked slowly around the table. If you don't tell me right now, I'll make sure that we miss this plane and every other." She sat firmly on his lap, put her arms around his neck, and began to nibble his shoulders as her hands drew long, sensuous circles on his back. She shifted her body seductively against his thighs, felt him stir, flicker against her buttocks. She moved her mouth to his ear; her tongue darted inside the tight shell, explored the complex whorls, indentations, and promontories. "Tell me," she demanded, laughing in soft delight as he squirmed beneath the tickling of her breath.

"Torturer," he moaned.

"Tell me!" Her tongue became more insistent; her hands moved to his nipples, the heel of her palm lifting them under her hard caress.

"Paris," he confessed at long last on a soft groan.

"Thank you." With a triumphant laugh, she tried to get to her feet.

"Oh, no, you don't!" Hard hands caught her hips. "You've just started something, wife, and you're not getting away without finishing it!"

"I thought we had a plane to catch," Emma reminded him slyly as he stood up, still holding her captive, to pull the towel from around his waist.

"We do. You'll just have to get ready double-quick." Sitting down again, he drew her firmly astride his lap.

"Gymnastics time, huh?" Emma murmured, resting her hands on his shoulders as he raised her hips, guiding her gently until they were joined.

"You asked for it, Emma mine," Mark responded softly, his eyes closing involuntarily as his head rested against the back of the chair.

"So I did." Rising slowly onto her toes, she withdrew her body before gently subsiding against him. A smile of sheer joy crossed his face, and her own expression melted with tenderness. It was her turn now to initiate their pleasure, to concentrate on Mark's reactions, to ensure that he was truly pleasured and to receive her own pleasure as an extension of his. This was the true togetherness of loving commitment, the ultimate sharing, and as they reached the glory of their finale, Mark raised his body to meet her, holding her steady in her precarious position with a firm hand at the small of her back, and the other on her hip. They met, fused, exploded in a champagne bubble of delight before she dropped into his waiting, encircling arms to receive the stroking caresses, the soft, nonsense endearments whispered against her skin as they returned to reality.

"Into the shower, my love, now!" Mark murmured urgently, lifting her to her feet. "We have to hurry."

"I want to take a bath," Emma announced with an effort.

"You bathe, I'll shower." Suddenly, he was all brisk efficiency, striding into the bathroom and rapidly filling the tub. Emma responded with equal, automatic speed.

"Mark, you do realize that with all this mystery and your haste to sweep me off into the night yesterday, I don't have my passport or my glasses?" Emma paused in her examination of the clothes in her suitcase. Mark had taken her totally by surprise at the end of their combined wedding and New Year's Eve party by quite literally carrying her out of the house at midnight, ignoring her squeaks of protest. He had told her to expect a honeymoon—somewhere—but had not prepared her for quite such a sudden departure!

"Your glasses are in your overnight bag and *I* have your passport," he responded equably, knotting his tie carefully in front of the mirror.

"Meg, I suppose?" Emma pulled out a soft heather-colored mohair skirt and a lavender cashmere sweater. Her question was purely rhetorical; she knew her live-in housekeeper/babysitter had conspired with Mark in this. "Oh, that reminds me." She pulled on a pair of pantyhose and then fastened her lacy bra. "I must call Sam before we leave, and we have to tell Meg where we'll be staying in Paris."

"Call Sam, sweet love, by all means, but you have neither the time nor the need for a long domestic discussion with Meg. Both she and Joe know our address. Joe said he wouldn't be going back to the dig until after we get home. So Sam has one parent on hand, in case of emergency."

Emma smiled slightly. Joe Richards, her ex-husband, was a devoted if usually absent father, and they had remained friends, but an utterly dedicated child psychiatrist wedded to her Boston hospital could not have remained married to an equally dedicated archaeologist with a passion for the lost Indian cultures of Peru.

"I promised Sam I'd call him every day." She reached for the phone. "That was before I realized you were going to whisk me off to the other side of the Atlantic. It's going to be an expensive business. I hope you realize that!" she added with a grin as the ringing signal sounded against her ear.

"Hello?" Meg's soft voice answered, and Emma felt the usual relaxation of maternal tension. Meg had moved in as resident housekeeper-in-chief and, most important, Sam's substitute mother when Emma had returned to work after maternity leave. Her divorce and Meg's marriage to Ted O'Rourke had somehow coincided. The house on the outskirts of Boston was far too large for just Emma and Sam, and it seemed both logical and appropriate to convert the huge basement into an apartment that now housed Meg, her husband, Ted, and their baby daughter, Anna. Ted ran his own construction business, and Meg ran the household, mothered Anna and Sam, and was Emma's closest friend.

"Hi, it's me," Emma responded.

"Having fun, Em?" Meg chuckled. "Sam's right here, bouncing like a rubber ball. Everything's fine, so don't start one of your long catechisms. You'll miss your plane and end up having the first quarrel of your married life!"

"Everyone but me seemed to know all about this honeymoon," Emma said, laughing. "Let me talk to Sam for a minute."

"Enjoy!" The soft laugh whispered down the wire and was instantly replaced by the excited shrieks of three-year-old Sam.

"Mommy, when you comin' home?"

"I've only just gone, darling," she protested lightly. "Mark and I are going on an airplane in a few minutes, to France."

"Yuss," the small voice responded matter-of-factly. "Mark told me you was goin' on a airplane, but it was a s'prise."

Emma choked. How typical of Mark! He would prepare the ground for the child as efficiently as he had done for everyone else, *and* ensure Sam's silence!

"What have you been doing today?" she asked, preparing herself for a rushed, excited catalog of the day's events. Sam's high-pitched voice burbled in cheerful recitation before he stopped abruptly: "'S Mark there? Wanna talk to him."

"He's right here, sweetheart. Say good-bye now. I'll talk to you again tomorrow." A noisy kiss exploded in her ear, and she returned it with equal enthusiasm before handing the phone to the tall figure standing quietly beside her.

"Hurry," Mark whispered. "You're not dressed yet." He turned his attention to the receiver, and she continued to dress rapidly, listening with a smile to his end of what could hardly be called a conversation.

"How many more of those are we going to have?" Mark asked as he finally put down the phone.

The mascara brush in her hand stopped in its efficient lengthening of her already fairly long lashes. "I hadn't even thought about it," she said slowly. "Would it bother you if I said my childbearing days were over?" This seemed rather an inappropriate moment to have such a serious discussion, she reflected, but then, such matters rarely came up at the ideal time.

"Yes, it would," Mark said frankly, "but I could live with it." His back was turned as he briskly closed and locked their suitcases. Emma frowned, trying to picture his expression. His voice was calm and even; his expression would be the same, she decided, although those warm brown eyes would probably be grave rather than merry, as they usually were.

"*Are* your childbearing days over?" The question came suddenly as he turned back to her. She had been right about his expression.

"I'm not sure," she said carefully. "As I said, I haven't given it much thought. It's going to take Sam awhile to adjust to having you around on a full-time basis, without adding sibling rivalry to the situation."

"Of course," he responded easily. "It was a general rather than a specific question. But the decision is definitely yours—whether it's 'when' or 'if.' " He gave her a slight smile and held out his arms. With an answering smile, she went to him, standing on tiptoe to kiss him with the light touch of a friend, the acknowledgment of a lover.

"Have you got the toothpaste, or have I?" he murmured into her hair.

Emma laughed softly. "You must have it. Last time I checked the bathroom, the only thing I could find was my toothbrush."

"Then, if you're quite ready, Mrs. Forrest, I suggest we move. Paris awaits."

2

"ONE OF THE nice things about eating croissants in a hotel bed is that you don't have to take responsibility for the crumbs," Emma declared one morning, two weeks later, licking her buttery fingers with considerable satisfaction.

Laughing, Mark reached for the thick, white china coffeepot on the bedside table. As he refilled their wide, shallow cups, he said teasingly, "I'm afraid, my sweet, that even though someone else will make the bed, the prospect of croissant flakes sticking to my skin is utterly repellent!"

"That doesn't surprise me." She grinned. "You're so neat and tidy." The soft glow of love that had filled and glorified these last wonderful days again engulfed her. They had been lovers for over a year now, but had never before spent this much time together. It had been Mark's methodical, calm, orderly manner that had first attracted her . . . Well, perhaps that wasn't quite true. But that quality had reassured her during the emotional onslaught of her initially reluctant realization that she found Mark Forrest totally compelling.

Mark had come to St. Anne's after working for four years at one of the top children's psychiatric hospitals in London and had brought with him a breath of professional fresh air that had instantly affected her. As she had come to know him, had heard the story of the tragic car accident that had killed his fiancée five years earlier and had sent him across the Atlantic, away from memories, her interest gradually turned into something quite different and infinitely disturbing. She had not wanted to admit this for a long time. Post-divorce life was far too bewildering and upsetting to allow for any further emotional complications. But eventually she had acknowledged her feelings, and Mark had quietly but with utter determination set about reducing her fears first to a mere pinprick and then to nothing.

"Neat and tidy, and very well organized," he concurred cheerfully, breaking into her musings. "And, since we're going our separate ways this morning in deference to our divergent tastes in art, we should institute a little organization into the proceedings."

"By all means," Emma murmured, pushing the tray off her knees and slithering down the bed.

"Emma, no! I've already told you I can't stand croissant crumbs." His voice shook with laughter.

"I'll brush them away," she offered hopefully.

"You'll get under the shower," Mark declared unequivocally. "I refuse to be sidetracked again this morning."

"I can't understand this passion for sight-seeing," she grumbled, swinging herself to the floor, reluctantly accepting the inevitable.

"My love, we have not done *that* much. Most of the time, you've kept me chained to the bed!" He was reaching into a dresser drawer for underclothes, his dancing eyes resolutely hidden.

"With silken manacles." She came up behind him, ran a provocative hand over the curve of his back.

Mark gave a low groan, straightened up, took her firmly by the hand, and led her into the bathroom. "*I* am going to spend the morning in the Louvre with David and Delacroix; *you,* Emma mine, are going to the Jeu de Paume. We will meet at Le Petit Coin de la Bourse at one o'clock—right?"

"No negotiation?"

"None whatsoever!"

With a sigh, she reached for her shower cap, tucking the mass of hair beneath the elastic before stepping behind the curtain.

Paris was always its own glorious self, whatever the time of year. This January was crisp, cold, and miraculously dry, and Emma paused in delight on the steps of the Musée du Jeu de Paume, breathing deeply of that indefinable, wintry Parisian smell—a curious mixture of roasting chestnuts, espresso, exhaust fumes from the constant, frenetic traffic, and a scent of perfume as an elegantly dressed woman whisked past her. The Place de la Concorde in front of her was, as always, a seething mass of honking cars, each one hurtling around the paved circle and then screaming to a halt inches from the car in front of it. Pedestrians, taking their lives into their hands, ran from one safe haven to another. The Arc de Triomphe stood, majestic, at the far vista of the Champs Élysées, stretching ahead of her.

Emma glanced quickly at her watch and pulled a rueful

face. She was going to be late. For such a relaxed individual, Mark had the most extraordinary obsession with punctuality. He was always at least ten minutes early for an appointment and deeply resented being kept waiting beyond the appointed time. These were the only occasions when his impeccable courtesy cracked, and Emma had watched, fascinated, the slight, uncomfortable squirmings of those unlucky enough to earn the polite raised eyebrow and the soft-spoken, sardonic disclaimer that, of course he didn't mind being kept waiting. It was going to be her turn now, even if she could find a cab driver willing to follow the traditions of a true Parisian! She ran down the steps, turned away from the long building that housed the museum, hurried through the now bare trees of the Tuileries until she reached the steps leading to the rue de Rivoli. She'd have a better chance of getting a cab there than in the Place de la Concorde. She jaywalked across the street at a run and stood outside W. H. Smith's, keeping watchful eyes on the stream of cars until she spied an empty cab and stepped out into the street with upraised hand.

"La Bourse, s'il vous plaît, rue Feydeau, aussi vite que possible," she instructed the driver swiftly, collapsing onto the back seat.

"D'accord, madame." The cabby grinned understandingly and then took off in a scream of rubber. She had found herself a gifted practitioner of the art of Parisian cab driving, Emma reflected, hanging on to the seat as the car swerved, coming within a hair's breadth of side-swiping another cab, then screaming to an impatient stop at an inconvenient traffic light.

Paying off the cab at the corner of the Place de la Bourse and the rue Feydeau, she glanced anxiously at her watch again; she was only fifteen minutes late. The small restaurant was packed with businessmen, mostly members of the Stock Exchange, indulging with quiet relish in that splendid tradition, a true Parisian lunch.

Emma noticed that, as usual in this district, the clientele was almost entirely male.

Mark was sitting at a small table beside the net-curtained window at the far end of the room. He was sipping a glass of *kir,* and another tulip-shaped glass of the pink-tinged apéritif stood beside the empty place opposite him. She paused for the barest instant to watch him, the firm, reflective profile, the broad shoulders clearly outlined beneath the superb cut of his moss-green sport jacket. At the same moment, as if by telepathy, he turned his head toward the door. The brown eyes smiled, but the straight eyebrows lifted slightly. Emma crossed the room quickly and bent to kiss his mouth.

"Sorry. *La circulation!*" She shrugged in swift, apologetic explanation.

"Really?" He rose politely, pulled out the table for her, eased her onto the padded bench with a firm, proprietorial hand in the small of her back. "It was the traffic, and not the Monets and the Manets?"

"A bit of both," she confessed with a smile. "I did leave the Jeu de Paume a little late, but if the traffic hadn't been quite so horrendous, I'd have made it almost on time."

"You're forgiven," he said gravely, but his eyes twinkled. "You enjoyed your morning, then?"

"Oh, yes!" she replied fervently. "I gorged myself on

Impressionists. It's funny you don't like them."

"Too much confectionery for my taste," he remarked cheerfully.

"Well, I bought a stack of posters. I hope you can live with them." Emma raised her glass of *kir,* and smiled over the rim.

"I'll survive." He smiled back and then turned toward the sommelier hovering beside his chair holding a bottle for his inspection. At Mark's quick nod, the wine steward drew the cork and poured a little wine into his glass. Mark sipped, nodded his approval, and sat back.

"What is it?" Emma asked as the waiter filled their glasses.

"Un bon Bordeaux," Mark replied easily. "St.-Estèphe, a very good year."

"But we don't know what we're eating yet." She frowned.

"You, Emma mine, are having coquilles Saint-Jacques à la provençale, followed by coq au vin," he stated calmly. "Since you were not here to order for yourself, I took matters into my own hands."

"Ouch!" Emma muttered.

Mark grinned. "Don't tell me you disapprove of my choice?"

"Of course not. I suppose I should be grateful you didn't pick something I detest."

"Come now, Emma," he said reprovingly. "I would never be *that* unkind!"

She laughed and stretched a hand across the table to take his, running her fingertips over his cuticles, stroking the prominent knuckles, turning the hand palm up, bringing it to her lips, nipping the soft, fleshy mound at the base of his thumb.

They had a leisurely, memorable lunch—the wine was excellent and the food delectable—made all the more pleasant by exchanging anecdotes of their morning apart interspersed with fond looks and endearments.

"So, what do you want to do this afternoon?" Emma asked as she took a quick sip of her espresso, shuddering with delight as the powerful essence hit her solar plexus.

"I rather thought we might take a little nap," Mark replied casually.

"What a waste of a beautiful afternoon," she murmured, keeping her eyes resolutely downcast.

"There are naps and naps, you know?"

"So there are. I was forgetting."

"You have a remarkably short memory, Mrs. Forrest," he responded, laughter rippling in his voice as he glanced over his shoulder to catch the waiter's eye.

The check appeared, Mark paid it, and within five minutes they were in a cab heading for the hotel nestling in a side street off the Champs Élysées, in the shadow of the arch.

"Take your clothes off, sweet," Mark whispered huskily as he shut the door behind them. "I'm going to take a shower; I want you ready for me."

Emma stood on tiptoe, wound her arms around his neck, nuzzled his cheek. "I'm ready now, my love."

"So am I." His teeth nipped her earlobe. "But this is one nap we're going to prolong. We're going to enjoy each other this afternoon, my sweet Emma. I'm in the mood to play!"

Laughing softly, she moved away from him, unbuttoning her shirt with slightly shaky fingers, watching as he shucked off his clothes before hanging them carefully in the closet. He was such an orderly man!

Mark disappeared into the bathroom, and Emma removed the rest of her clothes, then walked across to the window looking out on a small courtyard. Her gaze fell on the telephone on the far side of the king-sized bed. It wouldn't hurt just to make one quick call; she'd been away from St. Anne's for two weeks, and the occasional stab of anxiety, the need to reassure herself that all was well, had become somewhat urgent in the last few days. Just a quick call to the head nurse on night duty. She would be able to tell Emma if things were going smoothly. That was all Emma wanted, and she wouldn't be tempted to enter into a long, detailed discussion of day-to-day matters as she would if she called during Boston daytime and spoke to Delia Rivera, the head day nurse on the unit since its inception.

The thought was father to the action, and she dropped face down on the bed, reached for the phone, placed it on the cover beside her, and punched out the numbers. She heard the cascade of the shower, Mark's tuneless hum as the number rang. Just a two-minute call and she could enjoy the rest of her vacation with a light heart.

"St. Anne's." The operator answered with amazing speed.

"Extension three-oh-nine, please."

The next instant the phone was yanked out of her hand to be replaced with an unceremonious slam on its stand.

"Mark!" She looked up at him in stunned amazement.

What she saw in his face made her wriggle to the far side of the bed until her feet touched the floor again, and she rose swiftly.

"Just what did you think you were doing?" he demanded, moving around the bed toward her.

"I thought you were in the shower." Even as she muttered the words, Emma realized it was a totally inadequate explanation.

"I was, until I had this extraordinary feeling that you were up to something. Didn't we establish that there were to be no calls to the hospital during our honeymoon?" He advanced toward her, inexorably.

Mark lunged for her at the same moment that she leaped for the bed, and they tumbled together onto the firm surface. Emma suddenly found herself lying flat beneath him. His hands seized hers, palm against palm as he pinioned her wrists to the bed on either side of her head; his legs scissored hers into stillness, and she looked up into a face that bore all the signs of extreme annoyance—and something else. She struggled for a moment to identify the emotion and then knew—it was hurt. He was hurt by her apparent inability to live for three weeks just with him. Remorse flooded her, along with the realization that this was an occasion requiring desperate measures.

"Kiss me," Emma demanded.

"Kiss you?" His face and voice registered utter incredulity.

"Yes." She nodded vigorously. "Kiss me, right now."

There was a moment of total silence, and then suddenly Mark began to laugh. "You . . . you absolute . . . woman!" he exclaimed, as if it were the only word in the dictionary to describe her.

Emma grinned up at him, lying still, feeling his weight on her body as she awaited his next move.

"So you want to be kissed, do you, Dr. Grantham?" he asked eventually on a husky murmur.

"Mrs. Forrest does," she murmured back, her violet eyes locking with the deep brown eyes gazing down at her.

"I suppose I'm going to have to kiss the pair of you." A smile sparkled in his gaze.

"Sounds a bit schizzy to me," Emma whispered.

"Whose fault is that?"

Any response she might have made was stopped by his mouth. It was a totally un-Mark-like kiss—hard, demanding, possessive—and her body ignited with passion. She gave a tentative pull at her imprisoned hands, and his tightened. Sharp desire arrowed through her as she attempted an experimental twist of her lower body. His legs gripped hers in a hard, convulsive movement as he deepened the kiss, and excitement pierced her. This was a game they hadn't played before. She began to struggle in earnest, attempting to turn her body, to get leverage with her hips.

"Eel," he murmured laughingly against her mouth, dropping his full weight on top of her.

Strategy rather than force was the answer, she decided in the deepest recesses of her mind, feeling the life stirring against her thighs as she wriggled beneath him. Instantly, she became still, and her body went limp.

"Do you submit, Emma mine?" he whispered, raising his head.

She made an inarticulate movement of her head, felt him

relax in turn. Swiftly, she jerked her legs apart, taking advantage of his dropped guard to curl them around his back, her heels pressing into his buttocks with urgent demand.

"Never!" she laughed in delight and all-consuming passion.

"Impossible woman!"

And then he was inside her, responding to the urgent commands of her body, driving deeply as she rose to meet him, clutched him tightly with her inner muscles, saw him lose himself as glorious paroxysms engulfed them both.

They lay for a long time, still fused, his hands continuing to hold hers on the bed, until, finally, Emma opened her dazed eyes. She wriggled her hands, and this time Mark released them immediately. She ran a lazy caress over the body above her.

"I think I just died a little," she whispered in an awed voice.

"I think we both did," he whispered back, breath rustling against her neck. "*La petite mort,* the French call it."

"It's never happened like that before."

"We've never been so close to the edge of anger before." Gently, he disengaged himself, drew her tightly against him.

"I'm sorry," she murmured against his chest. "I'm just a workaholic, I guess."

"We have to get you unhooked," Mark said softly. "There's more in your life now than just St. Anne's and Sam."

"I know that, and I love you, my darling," she said, trying to burrow into his skin. "There's plenty of space; I just have to rearrange the furniture. I thought it would happen automatically, but it doesn't seem to."

"We'll make it happen, sweet," he promised. "I want a whole room to myself."

3

THE HOUSE BLAZED with light as the taxi drew up. The honeymoon had been glorious, but Emma's heart caught strangely, at the sight of her home—now Mark's home as well. She was scrabbling with the door handle before the cab had come to a stop. "Bring the teddy bear—it's in the trunk," she called to Mark over her shoulder, running up the sidewalk to the porch steps.

Mark laughed to himself as he watched her pell-mell dash and paid the cab driver. He had known Sam Richards for two and a half years and could easily understand Emma's urgency to get her arms around that square-faced, towheaded spark of humanity. He followed at a rather more leisurely pace with a suitcase and the enormous teddy bear that Emma had insisted on buying and whose presence had made their flight more than usually cramped. It took several trips to the porch to transport all their luggage, but he was in no hurry to interrupt, too soon, the mother-son reunion.

The door was open, and Mark stood for a moment watching the scene in the hall. Emma was on her knees smothering and smothered by her toddler's small, round body. The fair heads blended, Sam's a shade or two darker than his mother's. Mark felt a surge of longing to join in the scene. Perhaps it was time to remind them both of his presence, anyway. He put the bear behind him, out of sight—it was up to Emma when that would be produced—and stepped into the lighted circle of warmth.

"Hello, Sam."

The child looked up instantly, struggled out of his mother's arms, and ran to him. "'S Mark!" he yelled as if this were some sort of surprise, and leaped into Mark's arms. Mark inhaled deeply of the soft, soapy-clean baby smell of the child's skin, his hands feeling the warm body beneath the Superman pajamas. He had gotten the best package deal of the century when he'd finally induced Emma Grantham into marriage, Mark congratulated himself.

"Hi, you two." Meg, her *jolie-laide* face wearing its usual broad smile, came into the hall followed by a beaming Ted. "We were hoping the plane would be on time; I'd never have got Sam to bed."

"Doesn't look as if we're going to, anyway." Mark smiled, setting the excited little boy on his feet and waiting patiently for his turn to embrace Meg, who was presently exchanging hugs with his wife.

"Particularly when he sees what's outside." Emma grinned, releasing her friend and going to the door.

"Emma, that's outrageous!" Meg exclaimed at the sight of the very fat, four-foot-tall stuffed bear.

"Well, I was going to buy one for Anna as well," Emma replied wistfully, "but Mark didn't fancy sharing his seat with *two* of them, and I couldn't put them in the baggage compartment of the airplane because you can't wrap them up."

They all watched as Sam, with a look of awed delight, clasped around its large middle the toy that towered above him and staggered with it into the living room.

"Looks as if he's going to be occupied for a while," Meg observed. "You two want to eat? There's a casserole in the oven; Ted and I were about to start."

"My body clock is doing the strangest things right now," Emma responded. "I'm hungry, but I don't think I'm supposed to be. Am I?" She turned to Mark.

"You're entitled," he said cheerfully. "It's one o'clock in the morning, Paris time, and you didn't eat on the plane."

"I can't help feeling it's time someone was in bed," Mark commented several hours later as they sat in a state of sleepy repletion around the kitchen table.

Emma looked down at the chubby figure on her lap. Sam had been there for so long that his warm weight seemed to have become a part of her. "I guess you're right. Bedtime, Sam."

"Wanna be wiv you," Sam pronounced thickly through the thumb in his mouth.

Emma frowned thoughtfully. The circumstances were somewhat unusual, after all. "Go to sleep, then," she said softly, stroking his soft hair. "We'll take you up later." The child burrowed against her with a sigh and at last allowed his eyes to close. She glanced across at Mark. He raised his eyebrows slightly, gave a small shrug of acknowledgment. There were times when exceptions should be made.

She'd been back one week, and already it seemed as if she'd never been away, Emma thought as she walked briskly down the long institutional hallway on the ground floor of St. Anne's. She strode with an easy swing of her hips, in the direction of the wards and her own cheerful unit. The honeymoon had been a splendid idyll, but it was good to be back again, to hold the reins, to reassume the old routine—both work and domestic. Sam was being a little difficult, but that was an only-to-be-expected reaction to her absence and the anticlimactic aftermath of Christmas and New Year's. She and Mark were far too accustomed to dealing with children in various stages of confusion to be fazed by this particular testing three-year-old; however, she reflected, if Sam didn't come out of it soon, they were going to have to change their tactics. Indulgence could only go so far; it was time to call a gentle halt to the tantrums. Her quick step hesitated for a second as she saw the hospital's medical director ahead of her.

"Good morning, Dr. Grantham." His tone was silkily polite.

"Good morning, Dr. Jenner." Her response was equally polite, their mutual antagonism carefully hidden, as usual, under the courtesies.

She continued on her way. Jenner was a problem; he was of the old school and could see no merit in her concept of the children's psychiatric unit. As chief administrator of the hospital, he had a great deal of power and could make her life very difficult if he chose. So far, he had held his resentment in check, but she had an uneasy feeling that there were problems in store. Felix Markson, Jenner's predecessor, had been a very good friend and an utterly supportive boss. When Emma broke the bureaucratic rules in the interests of therapy, he had contented himself with a resigned sigh, had listened to her reasons, and had invariably requested simply that she document what she had done and state her reasons carefully. But then Felix liked her; Jenner didn't, and she had to admit his hostility was not without cause. His appointment had been purely political, and she had once been betrayed into articulating her lack of respect for his credentials. Somehow, he had found out—a malicious tongue somewhere in the institution had enjoyed the telling—but there was nothing she could do about it now. Everyone made mistakes, and she would have to live with this one.

Pushing the thought aside, Emma opened the door to the bright, busy dayroom.

"Hi, Em." A five-year-old with whom she had had an utterly draining play-therapy session the previous afternoon hurled himself at her knees, yesterday's fury forgotten.

"I hear you really enjoyed your honeymoon, hey, Em?" The question was accompanied by a suggestive, almost lascivious chuckle, and Emma, in the process of hugging the five-year-old, glanced up at her interlocutor. Fourteen-year-old Bella Atkins grinned at her before bending her heavily made up face again to the delicate task of applying scarlet polish to her long, talonlike fingernails.

"You've asked me that question every day since I came back, Bella," Emma said mildly. "My answer hasn't changed."

"Did Mark enjoy it?" The question brought a ripple of knowing laughter from the group of teenagers surrounding Bella.

"Ask him yourself, honey," she responded cheerfully, "and don't blame me if you get a snippy answer!"

She made her way to the nurses' station, shaking her head slightly. Bella was a major headache, and had to be handled with kid gloves as she perched constantly on the knife edge of explosion. "Why isn't Bella Atkins in school?" Emma walked into the small, bright room that resembled a kitchen with its shining Formica cabinets and countertops, stainless steel sink and stovetop.

"Running a fever again," Delia answered, raising her head from the chart in which she was entering a report.

"That girl runs fevers at the drop of a hat." Emma dropped her briefcase on the counter, then reached for the pile of internal mail waiting for her.

"They're genuine, though." Delia shrugged. "She doesn't get a chance to meddle with the thermometer before we take it."

But Emma didn't hear the head day nurse; her gaze was riveted on the memo from Jenner. "Owing to federal budget cuts, some reorganization of hospital programs has become necessary. The board of trustees and the hospital administration are working on this reorganization, and all unit heads will be notified in due course of the changes that they will be required to implement." She'd been expecting trouble, and this was it.

"I have to talk to Mark." Emma disappeared hastily into her small office off the nurses' station and reached for the phone. Mark had gone straight from home to his private practice in Cambridge this morning and wouldn't be in the hospital until after lunch.

Mark's receptionist answered the phone and told Emma that he was with a patient. "Ask him to call me when he's through," she responded, and replaced the phone. There was a team meeting in five minutes, and she'd have to put Jenner's memo on the back burner for a while. The phone rang in the conference room as she was pulling together the threads of their discussion. Delia reached for it, smiled in response to the voice at the other end, then handed the phone to Emma.

"Problems, sweet?" Mark's voice licked over her, bringing her skin to vibrant life.

"I don't know yet," she said hastily, conscious of the deliberately lowered eyes in the room around her. "Can you hold on a minute? I'll take this in the other room."

"Sure," he responded easily. There was a soft hum of amusement in his voice; he knew exactly why she had to go elsewhere.

Emma excused herself and hastened to her office. Even when the conversation was strictly business, she still found it impossible to talk with Mark on the phone in a roomful of people. His voice did the strangest things to her—things that she knew were nakedly revealed on her face.

"Are we alone?" he murmured huskily when she picked up the phone in her office. "I was just thinking about last night—you know those three little freckles you have on your—"

"Mark! Be serious for a minute," she choked. "This is work."

He sighed. "Very well, Emma mine, let's have it."

She read him the memo and was greeted with total silence. An uncomfortable thought struck her. "Mark, did you know about this?"

"I had an inkling," he replied eventually. "Money's tight, and everyone's looking to their budgets."

"Why didn't you warn me?" A strange, uneasy stab of something remarkably like betrayal shot through her.

"I didn't see any point in alarming you unnecessarily."

"Thanks," she said curtly, "but I've always believed that forewarned is forearmed."

"Don't make a big issue of this, darling," he said quietly.

"A big issue of what? That Jenner is about to play hatchet man, or that you knew about it and didn't tell me?"

"What are you doing for lunch?" His casual question ignored her tone.

"I have work to do," Emma said with an effort. "I'm not having lunch with anyone."

"You are now," came the firm response.

"I can't leave my desk."

"Then the mountain must come to Mohammed! I'll see you at one o'clock."

"Morning, everyone, or is it afternoon?" Mark's voice reached Emma as she sat at her desk. The general greeting to the roomful of children outside her office was received by a babble of voices.

"I *do* like your tie, Mark." Bella's voice separated itself from the cacophony. "The color exactly matches your eyes. Is it silk?" There was a short pause; then she heard Bella add coyly, "It *feels* like it."

"It is, and I'm glad you like it, Bella." His voice came smoothly, and Emma grinned, picturing the scene in the next room. Bella would be standing very close to Mark, her somewhat overripe adolescent bosom a little too close to his chest for comfort.

"I bet Em likes it." That same suggestive chuckle accompanied the words. "I bet she likes to take it off, too."

"There are some questions, Bella dear, that grown-up

people *may* ask, and some that they may not. But, of course, you're not quite grown up yet, are you'?" It was a very quiet put-down, but Emma, in the safety of her office, choked softly. One of these days, Bella Atkins would learn that sexual transference fell on stony ground with Mark.

"What's in those bags, Mark?" Timmy Baldwin's five-year-old voice piped suddenly, giving Bella, however inadvertently, the opportunity to withdraw gracefully from the ring.

"Lunch, Timmy," came the instant response. In her mind's eye, Emma saw Mark dropping to the child's level.

"For you and Em?"

"That's right," he responded cheerfully.

"Bet it's better than what *we* had." The childish voice carried a note of reproach.

"And what was that?" Mark was laughing, but with the child rather than at him.

"*Soggy* fried chicken," Timmy replied disgustedly, and there was a general chorus of groans. Emma's shoulders shook as she imagined the children's moues of distaste.

"My mom makes much better fried chicken."

Emma stopped laughing, listened intently for Mark's response.

"Why don't you get someone to help you write a letter, Timmy? Tell your mom you'd like fried chicken next time you go home on pass."

There was a short silence. Then the small voice said, "Who?"

"Maybe you could persuade Bella," Mark replied easily. "She writes very good letters."

Bravo, Mark! Emma applauded silently. Bella was

indeed very bright and articulate, but for some reason that Emma and Mark had not yet entirely fathomed, she chose to present quite another image to the world.

There was a mumbled "Maybe."

Then the half-open door of her office was pushed wide, and Mark stood in the doorway, smiling at her. She wanted to run to him, to bury her head in the crisp cotton of his brown shirt, to hear the steady thud of his heart, to feel those familiar but still exciting arms holding her safe, reassured. What on earth was happening—had happened—to independent Emma? She hadn't needed anyone's strength since she became an adult—not even Joe's. It wasn't that he had been unreliable, merely never around when she could have used an understanding presence. He'd broken no promises; they had just asked the impossible of two totally different personalities.

Mark pushed the door shut with a quick thrust of his hips as he came in, his hands full of brown bags.

"What have you got there?" she asked, sniffing eagerly.

"Sin," he grinned, bending to kiss the tip of her nose. "Egg rolls, shrimp toast, sticky spareribs, and fried wontons—not a nutritious vegetable in sight!"

"Mmm. Sounds marvelous," Emma murmured hungrily, beginning with swift fingers to open the cartons. Strangely, the ostensible reason for this lunch no longer seemed important. It was just a wonderful bonus to be together in the middle of the working day. Her sense of betrayal had vanished as soon as she had heard him in the dayroom. Mark would never do anything to hurt her; she knew that as surely as she knew she could never deliberately hurt him.

"So, Emma mine, you want to discuss things?" He wiped his fingers on the stack of napkins and sat back in the swivel chair, regarding her closely but somewhat uneasily.

"Only what you think is going on," she replied evenly. "I guess I overreacted this morning. That memo just came as such a shock."

He nodded, then crooked a finger. "Come over here, wife."

"Not in the office," she expostulated, rising nevertheless.

"Why not?" He grinned. "We always used to. I fail to see why marriage should make a quick kiss *verboten!*"

"It doesn't," she assured him, dropping onto his knee, wrapping her arms around his neck. "It just makes it more exciting. Strange, isn't it?"

She received no answer; he was far too busy.

A breathless few minutes later, Emma struggled upright, determinedly removed herself from Mark's encircling arms, and went to sit in her chair behind the desk.

"Now, Dr. Forrest, to business." She clasped her hands with businesslike efficiency on the desk blotter in front of her.

Mark chuckled. "Are you trying to intimidate me, Dr. Grantham?"

"I never try the impossible," she retorted smartly.

He laughed, but then became serious. "Jenner's out to make trouble for everyone, but particularly for you and the unit," he told her. "He's had orders to cut the overall budget, and I rather suspect he's going to use those orders to get his revenge. You're enemy number one."

"Yes, I know." Emma chewed her lip, a deep frown creasing her brow as she tapped her fingernails impatiently on the desk. "I should have been more discreet, but I don't think it would have made much difference in the long run."

"No, neither do I," Mark agreed briskly. "You scare the daylights out of him. You're far too independent and self-determining for the Jenners of this world, Emma mine! But it wouldn't matter if he only believed in the philosophy behind the kids' unit."

"Jenner is an archaic, chauvinistic abomination on the face of the psychiatric earth!" Emma declared roundly.

"Agreed! But there's not a damn thing either of us can do until we know exactly what we're up against. The ball is in his court, and you have to wait for him to play it."

"I guess so," Emma concurred with a sigh. "I just hate pacing back and forth nervously on my side of the net, waiting for him to serve."

"I'm here," he reminded her gently. "You're not alone, sweet."

"I know," she said softly, smiling. "Still it takes a bit of getting used to."

"Well, I would appreciate it if you could start getting used to it!" Mark tossed their plates and the empty cartons into the wastebasket as he got to his feet. "I have to run, Emma." He gave her a searching, anxious look. "Ride with this one, kid. There's nothing you can do at the moment."

"No." She nodded. "What time will you be home?"

"I have a patient at five o'clock—so I should be there about six-thirty." He dropped a light, brushing kiss on her eyelids as he moved toward the door. "Oh, by the way." He paused, hand on the doorknob. "If Sam is going to continue playing the *enfant terrible,* we're going to have to come up with something new."

"I'm working on it." She smiled.

"Mmm. You're not alone on that one, either, Emma mine."

The door closed, and she sat looking at it thoughtfully for a moment. Learning how to share problems as well as joys was proving a lot more difficult than she had anticipated. Mark never pushed her, but if he didn't come right out and offer to help, she usually did her own worrying and problem-solving. Old habits died hard, of course, and she was trying, but she was beginning to get the feeling that he was becoming just a little impatient.

It was seven o'clock before Emma wearily parked her yellow and black striped Renault, which she and Mark had nicknamed "the bee," in front of the house. Mark's BMW already stood a few cars up. She had not intended to be this late, but her session with one particularly difficult new admission had run beyond the scheduled hour. It was against hospital rules, of course, to prolong sessions, but no one would know unless somebody read her case notes, and her reasons for doing so were unarguable.

She climbed the porch steps, pushed open the door into total silence—no scampering feet, no ecstatic yells of "Mommy! Mommy!" No small boy hurling himself into her arms. Frowning, she headed for the kitchen, where all domestic answers would be found.

Meg was sitting in the rocker by the wood-burning stove, reading a story to her daughter Anna; Ted was deep in the newspaper as he ate his supper with methodical concentration. They both looked up as she entered.

"Hi, there," Emma said, smiling. "Where's Sam?"

"Upstairs with Mark," Meg replied carefully. "I think Mark's giving him a bath."

Emma opened the refrigerator, took out a bottle of pouilly-fuissé, reached into the cabinet for glasses, filled three, and passed them around. "What happened?"

"How did you guess?" Meg took a quick sip of wine.

"You could cut the atmosphere in this house with a knife," Emma said succinctly.

"Mark got home about half an hour ago and walked into the middle of a true Sam Richards tantrum," Ted informed her.

"I wasn't home," Emma said miserably.

"It wasn't that, Em," Meg reassured her quickly. "Sam's used to your being late, so long as you call him, and you did."

Emma nodded. "Then what was it?"

Meg shrugged. "I don't know exactly—part of the pattern of the last week or so. He was fine while you were away, and most of the day he's his usual sunny self. But as evening comes on, and he gets ready for your return . . ." She made a gesture of inarticulate frustration with her free hand. "I can't explain it, Em. It's your field of expertise and Mark's, not mine."

"Oh, Meg!" Emma squeezed her friend's shoulders. "You know that's not so. You understand Sam as well as I do—sometimes I think even better. Tell me what happened before I join them."

"Sam wasn't interested in finishing his milk," Meg explained. "He had the usual choice—juice or milk—and asked for milk. Then, after two sips, he decided he'd rather have juice. The rules are clear; he knows once he's asked for something, he's not to change his mind."

"Sure," Emma agreed swiftly. Sam was expected to make his own choices in these small matters and then to abide by them. "So?"

"So he happened to be throwing his milk across the kitchen when Mark walked in," Meg explained briefly.

"And then what?" Emma asked uneasily. She trusted Mark's instincts and expertise absolutely, but she couldn't deny the shaft of anxiety, the sense that dealing with Sam was primarily her responsibility—but then, of course, she hadn't been here!

"Mark just scooped him off his chair, encouraged him to mop up the mess as well as a three-year-old could, and took him upstairs. The last thing I heard was the sound of the tub filling." Meg gave her a lopsided smile.

"He wasn't angry?"

"Sam was. Mark wasn't, but he wasn't particularly indulgent either," Meg replied calmly.

Emma nodded thoughtfully. "We'd talked a bit about changing our tactics—finally cracking down. This was clearly the moment." She reached for another glass, filled it with wine and made for the door, holding the two wineglasses carefully. "I don't suppose Mark has drowned the little imp!"

"I gathered that they were going to have a little chat." Meg grinned.

"I think I'd better make this a tripartite chat." Emma grinned back. "You know what they say about no peace for the wicked!" She heard Meg and Ted's responding laughter as the door swung closed behind her.

At the head of the stairs, she paused; Sam's shrill squeal

of delight reached her from the bathroom down the hall.

Both her son and Mark were in the large old-fashioned tub. Sam shrieked, "Mommy! Mommy's back, Mark! Mark and me, we's playin' ships." He struggled out of the bathwater, arms outstretched, wet and dripping, to his feet.

Emma set the glasses on the shelf above the sink, grabbed a towel hastily, wrapped the small, rounded body, and swung it to the floor, kneeling to dry him. Chubby arms reached around her neck and, as she cradled Sam, her eyes met Mark's over the blond head.

"My turn soon?" He smiled.

"Mmmm." She reached for a glass of wine, handed it to him. "Drink that, and I'll have you dry and in bed in no time!"

"Can't wait," he murmured, sinking into the water with a deep sigh of contentment.

It was a good twenty minutes later when she returned to the bathroom, having deposited a sleepy, pajamaed Sam into bed, read to him, and sung the ritual lullaby, wishing, as always, that she could carry a tune.

"You still in that water?" She grinned, beginning to undress. "You're going to get all wrinkly."

"I've been waiting for you," Mark said plaintively. "I think I've emptied the hot-water tank, trying to keep the temperature acceptably warm." He extended a long foot; the toes curled over the spiked knobs of the faucet, and steamy water poured into the already full tub. "Not quite," he smiled happily.

"We are about to flood the floor," Emma said matter-of-factly as she slithered into the water, facing him.

"Two mopping-up jobs in one evening? Oh, well, those

are the breaks." He pushed his feet beneath her, curling his toes against her bottom. Emma wriggled deliciously.

"I can't talk about that problem seriously if you don't behave yourself," she said severely.

"I don't think there's that much to talk about," he responded, reaching for the soap, lifting her leg, and beginning to wash her foot. "Sam and I already sorted a few things out."

Emma sighed contentedly as he massaged her toes with firm, soapy fingers. "Like what?"

"Just a little limit-setting," he murmured, lifting her foot to his mouth, running his tongue between her toes.

"That feels so good!"

"I like your feet," he stated coolly. "They're so long, and narrow, and you have such pretty little pink toes."

She gurgled softly. "Just be serious for a minute, will you? Oh . . . !" She gave up the unequal struggle as his palms slipped up her leg, flattened against her inner thigh; his fingertips reached, felt intimately, knowingly.

Mark laughed with pure pleasure, caught her waist and drew her up the length of his legs until she was sitting astride his thighs. "Just as a matter of interest," he asked as he began to soap her throat, her shoulders, "what kept you? You said you'd be back by six."

"Jerry Donovan threw a fit," she explained. "I couldn't end the session until we'd worked through it."

He nodded, running soapy hands down her arms, stroking her wrists, feeling for the now fast-beating pulse. You don't think that perhaps it might be better to schedule sessions that could prove difficult for some time other than the end of the day?"

"What are you trying to say, Mark?" Emma frowned. He was saying one thing to her with his hands, but quite another with his voice, which was curiously solemn.

"I'm trying to say, my darling, that I think we need to regulate things a little more than we are right now." He reached for one creamy breast. "We could ensure that, barring emergencies, we get home by six-thirty. And that, on alternate days, one of us gets home by six o'clock."

"I get the strangest feeling that you're criticizing me. I'm not generally considered a bad mother," she said tightly, trying to pull back from the hands cupping her breasts, to ignore the flood of sensation as his fingers teased her hard, wanting nipples.

"Now, you're being just a mite foolish," he murmured, his lips following his fingers.

"I'm not!"

He raised his head, moved his hands to her back, running a delicious caress down its length. "Sweet, I'm not criticizing you. I'm merely pointing out that since we are now married, we can change the pattern of our lives to provide Sam with a little extra-special attention. When he was a baby, it was all right for Meg to provide the practical mothering and for you to come home when you could in time to tuck him in. But he's getting bigger day by day. He goes to bed later and is wider awake in the early part of the evening. He needs parental time then."

"Stop touching me," Emma said desperately. "I can't concentrate on what you're saying when you're giving me two different messages."

"I'm giving you *one* message," he asserted, continuing with the gentle stroking. "You're just missing it. I love you,

Emma mine. I love you with my body and with my mind, and that's the only message I'm giving you. You're no longer a single parent juggling job, house, and child all by yourself. We share all three, and the load can be halved to everyone's benefit—particularly Sam's."

"Then you *are* saying I'm at fault," she cried miserably. "I stay too long at work and don't spend enough time with Sam."

"*Before* our marriage, you did what was necessary," he said with gentle emphasis. "It is no longer necessary. Turn around now."

"No! I won't let you lecture me and then make love to me," she protested.

"I wasn't lecturing you," he said with a sudden, wicked grin. "But I think it's time you learned to do as you're told!" With that he pulled himself to his feet, heedless of the cascade of water pouring over the rim of the tub. Hard hands grasped her waist, lifted her inexorably onto the bath mat where he followed instantly. He wrapped her in a large, fluffy bath sheet and vigorously rubbed her dry until her skin glowed.

"Now, Emma mine, we'll finish this in bed. Let's see you move!"

"That was some guilt trip you laid on me," Emma murmured much, much later, curling against Mark's virile, fragrant warmth. The subject was still not closed to her satisfaction, and she had never been one to tolerate unfinished business.

Mark rolled onto his side, propped himself up on one elbow looking down at her. "We seem to be having a most unusual problem," he observed with a frown. "Either I have lost my ability to make my meaning clear or you have lost your perceptive faculties. Let me try just once more. There is nothing the matter with Sam that a little firm handling at this juncture won't cure. He's a perfectly well adjusted, stable, contented little boy—and you don't need me to tell you that."

"So what *is* all this about?" Emma queried.

"It's about the three of us," he said carefully. "The fact that we are now a family—that you are no longer a single parent."

"I know that." She frowned, puzzled.

"Well, you may know it, but we aren't adapting our lifestyle accordingly," Mark stated firmly. "Our weekday evenings are a mess! We're both exhausted when we get home. There's time for a quick parenting session—if that—with Sam before he goes to bed. After that, we scrabble around for something to eat, and then one or both of us spend the next couple of hours writing up case notes or something. How many times, after we'd planned to go out in the evening, have you turned up at eight o'clock with a pile of charts?"

"Too often," she agreed reluctantly. "It's just that I'm so used to working in the evening. Once Sam was in bed, there weren't any other calls on my time."

Mark said nothing, just looked steadily at her until finally she sighed, smiling slightly. "I've sprung my own trap, haven't I?"

He nodded. "There are *now* other calls on your time. I don't think I'm particularly demanding, and to a certain extent we're both slave-driving ourselves with work, but

I'm willing to make some concessions. Are you?"

"Yes, I guess so," she said thoughtfully. "But I don't see how I can cut down on my case load. I don't manufacture work; someone has to do it."

"There's such a thing as delegating authority," he said quietly. "You have psychiatric social workers and psychologists on the team, but you still mastermind every aspect of the treatment for each patient in the unit, in addition to handling the administration of the program."

"I don't mastermind the treatment for your patients," she protested.

"I should damn well hope not!" He grinned. "But I have five to your fifteen. If I cut down on the private practice a bit, I can take some more. What do you think?"

"Do you really want to do that?"

"Emma, I've just said that we will both have to make some adjustments if we're going to make this marriage more than two adults and a child passing like ships in the night five days a week!"

She raised her eyebrows. "That's a rather harsh assessment of our situation, isn't it?"

"I don't think it is," he responded calmly. "It's what's happening at the moment."

Emma absorbed this in frowning silence for a while before nodding slowly. "You're right; we need to get organized. We could start right now by thinking about dinner. I'm famished!"

Mark laughed, and there was an unmistakable note of relief in the deep, rich sound. "Do you want to go out? Or shall we see what Mother Hubbard's cupboard can offer?"

"It's probably a bit bare," she said with a rueful grin, "but

I'm too lazy and relaxed to get dressed again. We've got lots of eggs and cheese."

"Cheese omelets coming up," he said cheerfully, getting to his feet. "Stay put, won't be long."

Emma swung her feet to the floor. "No, I'll help . . ." She subsided onto the pillows again as Mark fixed her with a gimlet eye. "I don't know what's come over you this evening, Mark Forrest," she grumbled. "You're exhibiting an alarming tendency to become very bossy."

"On occasion, Emma mine, you need to be bossed," he observed coolly.

"What a chauvinistic remark!" Emma exclaimed.

"Not at all," he responded, pulling on his robe. "We all need it sometimes. Tonight, it just happens to be your turn."

Marriage, Emma reflected as the door closed behind him, was indeed a curious business. All of a sudden one found oneself sharing one's personal space. She had felt several times this evening that Mark had been invading hers—an uncomfortable feeling that she now realized was actually the result of a misinterpretation on her part: He had not been invading, merely taking his rightful place.

4

"WELL, THAT'S THE situation, Dr. Grantham. I'm very sorry, but all units are going to have to make drastic reductions in service."

Emma sat still, her face impassive, as she listened to Dr. Jenner's smooth tones delineating the cuts that would affect her unit. They weren't so much cuts, she thought bitterly, as a complete massacre. A siren wailed outside, and Emma contemplated the destruction of everything she had worked for in the last three years. But Jenner was still waiting for her response, and she had to say something that sounded neutral, that revealed nothing of her inner pain and sense of desolation; she would not give him that satisfaction.

"I understand your position, Dr. Jenner," she said smoothly, and had a moment of malicious pleasure as she saw surprise flash in his eyes. "I'll need some time to work out modifications in our program. I hope that won't be a problem."

"Not at all," he replied, recovering quickly. "I'll be glad to have your *suggestions* by the end of the week." He placed heavy emphasis on the word "suggestions," and Emma fought down her fury. The battle was now out in the open: She wasn't even going to be allowed to make definitive modifications to the program, just suggestions.

She rose and hold out her hand. "I appreciate your discussing this with me personally, Dr. Jenner. You will have my *recommendations* within days."

Jenner's hand touched hers briefly, and once outside the room she rubbed her palm against the seat of her corduroy skirt, desperate to remove the feeling of clammy contamination from her skin.

"I don't want any calls, Lyn," she said brusquely to her secretary as she entered the anteroom outside her administrative office on the third floor. "If there's a patient problem, you'll have to find Mark or Delia." She was only vaguely aware of Lyn's astonished gaze as she marched into her office, pulling the door shut with uncustomary, unnecessary force.

A long time later she heard the door open. "I said I didn't want to be disturbed!" She didn't take her eyes off the paper in front of her.

"Did you, now?" the voice drawled, and then she looked up. Mark was leaning against the door, the power in his body an almost tangible force in the room.

Emma sighed. "So you heard?"

"Of course. What are you going to do about it?"

"I'm resigning." She indicated the paper on the desk in front of her.

"Don't be, an idiot, Emma. Jenner will accept your resignation quicker than you can write it."

"You don't understand, Mark," she replied wearily. "I'm not threatening resignation, I *am* resigning."

"Over my dead body!" Mark whisked the letter from her desk and held it out distastefully between finger and thumb.

"Mark, give that back!" Emma leaped to her feet, leaning over the desk to reach for the letter as he held it away from her grasping fingers.

"Sit down, darling," he said with infuriating calm. "I will not! Just give that back, Mark Forrest. This has nothing to do with you."

"Do as I say!" he thundered, and with a gasp she plopped back into her chair. "That's better." He strode to the door, opened it, spoke to the startled, wide-eyed Lyn, who had clearly heard the booming instruction from within. "No calls, Lyn, unless it's a home emergency," he directed with a disarming smile. Closing the door firmly, he turned back to his wife.

Emma, still trying to recover from the shock of being shouted at, looked at him with a mixture of indignation and resentment. "There was no need to bark at me like that."

"I was just being husbandly," he observed equably, perching on the edge of her desk, still holding the paper.

"It's considered husbandly to yell at one's wife as if she were a recalcitrant dog?" she queried sardonically.

"You were not behaving like yourself. Professional expertise indicated that a short, sharp shock was in order." He smiled tranquilly. "Now, do you want to discuss this here, or shall we go home?"

"I don't think there's anything to discuss," she said tiredly, sitting back in her chair. "I don't think you understand, love. I've had enough of fighting. If it were anyone but Jenner . . ." She shrugged hopelessly.

"So, the kids are going to lose their last advocate?" Mark questioned conversationally.

"Damn you," she said softly. "Why did you have to bring that up?"

"Because it's the real issue, as well you know," he responded. "Are you going to tear up this piece of garbage, or am I?" He flicked the draft of her resignation with a disdainful forefinger.

With a resigned shake of her head, she held out her hand, took the sheet, ripped it into shreds, and dropped them into the wastebasket. "That bastard Jenner," she exploded suddenly. "He was so smug, Mark; you have no idea!"

"Go wash your face and put on some more makeup. You look as if a truck had just hit you." Mark reached for the phone. "I'm going to call Meg and tell her we'll be late."

"Why? Where are we going?"

"In search of crab." He grinned. "By the time you've hammered the hell out of a dozen or so, you'll be able to deal with this more clearly."

"A bit of play therapy, you mean?" Suddenly, she was able to smile again. She wasn't going to have to deal with this alone.

"Seems appropriate." His responding smile was soft, tender, full of the promise of shared burdens.

"So much for you, Dr. Jenner!" Emma declared forcefully, bringing her wooden mallet down on an innocent crab resting on the brown paper-covered table in front of her.

Mark laughed. "Atta girl!" And then he became serious. "If you're ready for some constructive suggestions, as opposed to this therapeutic bashing of dead crab, I have a couple."

Emma sucked some succulent sea-tasting meat from a claw and looked across the table. "Ready."

"Okay. First: You may not be able to keep the unit in its present form, but you can try to mold the changes to a format *you* choose. It'll be you against Jenner convincing the board, and you'll have the edge. Your track record, sweet, in spite of your somewhat maverick tendencies, is regarded with a degree of awe by our financial masters." He smiled with an almost proprietorial pride, reached for her sticky hand, and squeezed it firmly. "Now, second: You know about the international convention in London, in April?"

Emma nodded. "You're giving a paper on autism."

"Right. I think you should submit a paper, too—a description of the unit and its philosophy. It's a highly prestigious convention. If they accept your paper, St. Anne's is going to have a tough time explaining why they want to dismantle the unit."

Emma took a long time before she answered him, concentrating on extricating the last morsel of meat from the crab in her hands. "I haven't done anything academic for ages," she said eventually.

"You won't have a problem getting back into the swing of it," he asserted firmly. "And I've finished my paper, so if you're willing to accept my help . . ."

"Willing?" She smiled softly, raising her eyebrows.

"Let's go!" Mark drained his beer glass and waved a hand at the waitress.

"Why the hurry?" she murmured, her eyes dancing with mischievous invitation.

"I want you," he told her matter-of-factly, tossing a credit card beside the check. "I want you naked and soft and pliant. Dr. Grantham is a most exhilarating companion in the daylight hours, but right now I want to go to bed with my wife."

"What a thankless task it is, to try to seduce someone else's husband," Emma sighed, reaching for her purse.

"Well, when you have a wife like mine, I'm afraid no one else is going to have a chance." Mark signed the check, tore off the carbon, smiled sweetly at the fascinated waitress standing, all ears, beside the table as he handed her the original.

"I'm not sittin' next to him," the tall, leather-jacketed teenager announced firmly, glaring at his long-limbed compatriot sprawled, with a smirk that could only be called

59

insolent, in the chair next to the only vacant seat in the room.

Emma sighed. "José, I don't care whether you sit next to Mario or not. Just put your body in a chair, please. We're late starting this session as it is."

José looked slowly and deliberately around the room, making his point that there *were* no other chairs.

"Would someone please change places?" she asked wearily. Instantly, the entire circle of twenty children, ranging in age from five to fifteen, leaped to their feet and began a game of musical chairs, their delighted giggles providing a somewhat less than musical accompaniment.

Emma glanced across the dayroom at Delia, who shook her head sympathetically. Ordinarily, Emma would have been amused by the scene, but the strain of the last few days was beginning to tell, and the threat to the unit was keeping her, at the moment, on a precipice of nail-biting anxiety.

"Just hold it right there!" Her voice cut through the excited babble sharply, much more forcefully than was her custom, and an astonished silence fell. The children resumed their original seats, leaving the problem of José and Mario still unresolved.

"Please, sit down, José," she requested politely. This business had gone on quite long enough: she had been on the verge of allowing the weekly group session to get out of hand, and fatigue and anxiety were no excuse.

Tension crackled around the group as José hesitated. The boy was on the verge of rebellion. She met his glowering black eyes steadily. Having initiated a confrontation, she could not afford to lose it publicly. Seconds ticked past, and the silence lengthened. Recognizing the point at which José was uncertain what to do in order to save face, Emma said quietly, "Why don't you just sit there for a moment? Perhaps we should put what's between you and Mario at the top of our agenda this afternoon?"

"That's got nothin' to do with anyone here." Mario spoke up for the first time as José reluctantly sat beside him.

"Does everyone else agree with that?" Emma looked calmly around the circle of intent faces.

"No." It was Jerry Donovan who had spoken, and she felt her fatigue recede under the explosion of excitement. Donovan had never opened his mouth—except to give an obvious, bored yawn—at any group session before. "When them two fight, we all get involved. It ain't s'posed to be that way—we're s'posed to bring family problems to Em or Mark, or someone. But with José and Mario, everyone else gets into the battle—just 'cause they're cousins, and Mario's uncle had a deal with José's father and—"

"Sorry to disturb you, Dr. Grantham." The smooth, malicious voice brought Emma's head up sharply; she was furious that someone had had the lack of professionalism to break into such a discussion. Surely not even Jenner would do such a thing? But he had. He was standing outside the circle with a group of "sightseers," as the hospital staff always called the groups of interested visitors who were taken on tours of carefully selected units. Emma swung herself off the window ledge where she had been sitting with the informality that characterized their sessions. Somehow she had to control the white core of rage melting inside her.

"We have visitors," she said pleasantly. "We'll have to

discuss this some more another day. Delia wants to talk about arrangements for Pete's birthday party next week. If you really want to barbecue in this weather, someone's going to have to clean that grill outside. As I remember, there were no volunteers after Labor Day; it's going to be a lot tougher now."

A self-conscious giggle ran around the room, answering her easy laugh, and then Jerry Donovan, surprisingly, said, "I'll do it."

"Good for you, Jerry." Emma walked briskly across the room to the rather bewildered-looking group of visitors.

"Maybe you'd like to come into the 'quiet room,'" she said firmly. It was definitely not a request, and they followed her down the wide hallway to the large room at the back of the unit.

"I have a feeling we interrupted something rather important, Dr. Grantham. I'm sure I speak for all of us when I say how sorry I am."

Emma looked at the speaker and felt some of the anger leave her. Charles Graves was chairman of the board—the man whose initial support for her proposal for this unit had helped carry it through the tangled webs of bureaucracy to fulfillment.

"That's quite all right, Mr. Graves," she responded politely. "Our weekly meetings were considered sacrosanct in the past, but these are changing times." It was a direct challenge, which he acknowledged with a narrowing of his eyes and an almost imperceptible nod.

"Can I answer any questions?" Emma smiled with only superficial warmth, but her invitation was nevertheless taken up enthusiastically, and for the next thirty minutes she responded to the sharp, pointed questions of the group of mental-health researchers. Public relations was part of her job—more so now than ever.

As the observers thanked her for her time and prepared to leave, Charles Graves laid a restraining hand on the stiff arm of the medical director. "I'd like to talk to Dr. Grantham for a minute, Jenner. Why don't you continue the tour and I'll catch up?"

Dr. Jenner had no choice, but his eyes darted liquid venom at Emma as he ushered the others out of the room.

"You've made yourself a powerful enemy there, Emma," Graves said thoughtfully as he closed the door.

Emma was silent. There was no point denying it.

"I understand you've submitted a request to be allowed to address the board?" the chairman went on.

"I'm amazed Jenner put the request through!"

He laughed. "Come now, Emma, that's unworthy of you. Jenner's no fool, you know."

Emma shrugged and laughed, too. "You're right. It would be easier if he were."

"Well," Graves resumed briskly, "the next board meeting is on Tuesday. How much time should I allot you?"

Emma bit back an exclamation. Tuesday was less than a week away! But she was being offered an opportunity, and there wouldn't be another one.

"Thirty minutes, minimum," she replied decisively.

"I can give you an hour, between three and four o'clock," was the swift reply. "Get Mark to come with you. Two opinions are always more persuasive than one."

Emma frowned. "Jenner's bound to bring up conflict of interest if Mark comes."

"I hope he'll have more sense," Graves said grimly. "Only a fool would question Mark's objectivity when it came to a professional opinion on the kids' unit."

"And, as you've just said, Charles, Jenner is no fool," Emma said demurely.

"Right." Charles Graves gave her a tiny smile and left the room.

5

"How are you feeling, Em?" Delia looked up with a sympathetic smile as Emma walked into the nurses' station on Tuesday afternoon.

"I'm shaking like a leaf," Emma said ruefully, holding out her hands and examining them critically.

"Well, you look very cool." Delia considered her friend, taking in the tailored lavender linen shirtwaist, the slim-heeled sandals, and the elegant, though severe, chignon.

"I'm trying for a schoolmarm image." Emma grinned, pulling out her reading glasses and perching them on the end of her nose. "What do you think?"

"Jenner won't be fooled for a moment, and neither will Charlie Graves," Delia said with an irreverent chuckle.

"I suppose you're right," Emma sighed, perching on a high revolving stool at the counter. "But it's what's in here that counts." She patted the manila folder in front of her. "If the trustees are willing to open their ears to this, we won't have a problem."

"That's what I like to hear, kid, a bit of the old fighting spirit!" Mark rested his hand briefly on her shoulder as he came into the room. Emma gazed at his superbly cut three-piece suit, the slate-gray fabric taking on a silky texture in the light. The pale blue shirt and charcoal-gray tie she knew were silk, having bought them herself.

"You look magnificent," she breathed, forgetting Delia's presence for an instant.

"May I return the compliment? Nothing but the best for the kids' unit." He gave her a long, slow appraising look. "Nervous, sweet?"

"Sick as a dog," she replied frankly. "But I'll be all right once we're in there."

"Come on, then, Dr. Grantham, let's throw ourselves to the wolves."

Emma slid off the stool in response to the light pressure on her elbow. "Wish us luck, Delia."

"All the luck in the world." Delia smiled, holding up crossed fingers.

"Hold my hand," Emma whispered insistently as they rode the elevator to the sixth floor. He took it firmly.

"It's like ice," he murmured. "This isn't going to be as bad as you think. Relax!"

"I prefer to be prepared for the worst." She smiled ruefully.

"As if I didn't know." He laughed softly, leading her out of the elevator as it came to a shuddering halt.

"Mr. Graves said for you to go straight in." The young woman behind the desk got to her feet and moved to the large oak door leading to the boardroom.

Mark released Emma's hand and stood courteously aside as she walked in, her eyes and mind instantly assessing the faces around the smooth black oval of the table. She knew them all, had talked to them all before on similar occasions;

but this time, the only ones whose reactions she could predict were Jenner and Graves.

"Dr. Grantham, Dr. Forrest, I'm so glad you could be with us this afternoon." The chairman's voice was neutrally polite as hc indicated two empty seats on opposite sides of the table. Emma felt a totally unanticipated stab of desolation. Mark would be too far away from her! But his eyes smiled at her as he took his seat, telling her that she could do this, that she didn't really need him. She smiled back at him openly—and to hell with the others in the room! She *did* need him, and would tell him so.

Her tension and nervousness suddenly disappeared. This was like taking an examination when you knew you were well prepared; the apprehension vanished once you saw what was before you and accepted that from now on there was an inevitability about success or failure.

"Dr. Grantham? The ball is in your court." The chairman's soft invitation prompted her to open her folder, and take her glasses from her purse.

"I'm grateful for your time, ladies and gentlemen," she said, directing a polite smile around the table.

Then Jenner's voice interrupted her low-key beginning. "I understand, Dr. Grantham, that you have submitted a paper on the children's unit to the psychiatric convention in London."

"That is correct," she replied.

"Didn't it occur to you that the board members were entitled to see a copy of that paper before its submission?" Jenner sat back heavily in his chair, trying unsuccessfully to hide his complacency at the disapproving shiftings and whisperings that greeted his disclosure.

I think, Jenner, that you've just played an ace before you were ready, Emma thought, excitement surging through her at the scent of a challenge. She fought it down; it was all too easy to underestimate an opponent, whether it was over a bridge table or in the boardroom. However, the ace had to be trumped, and she proceeded to do so.

"My paper, Dr. Jenner, is purely academic. In it, I do not identify the hospital or the unit. I have simply described a method of treatment and backed it up with statistics that are no secret to anyone in this room. I have copies of the paper right here." She patted the stack of papers in front of her. "I'd be happy to leave them with you and retire while you read it; I can answer any questions later." She delivered the coup de grâce with a delicacy that even she, in this highly charged atmosphere, found satisfying.

Mark watched the small, heart-shaped face across from him. She was looking, as he had expected, very intent and serious, those gorgeous, expressive eyes hidden behind the formidable glasses. Her hands were quite still as they rested on the folder on the table. He wondered why he had felt nervous for her. Emma never had any problem dealing with this sort of challenge. Her only difficulty was that she didn't suffer fools gladly. No reason why she should, of course, he reflected. That razor-sharp mind, that utter dedication and willingness to push herself to the limits of her endurance, didn't allow for too much tolerance when either a colleague or a superior slipped, whether through negligence or indolence.

But Charles Graves was continuing. "That won't be necessary, Emma." The chairman used her first name, an unusual procedure on these formal occasions, but one that aligned him firmly on her side. "We'd like to read it later, as a matter of academic interest." He laid careful stress on the last phrase. "What we need from you now are your arguments for maintaining the unit in its present form, given the necessary budget reorganizations."

"It cannot be kept in its present form," Emma said firmly, and watched with satisfied interest the surprise her remark created. "I am accepting that we have to cut costs. What I have here are some proposals for trimming expenses without making drastic changes in the type and quality of the treatment we offer." She paused and looked around the table, assessing the reactions.

"We're all ears, Emma," Charles Graves said with a slight smile.

Emma explained her new proposals concisely, describing the factors that made the unit a success and emphasizing quietly but deliberately the importance of that success on the political and financial support for the hospital. She glanced quickly across the table. Mark appeared calm and relaxed. So far she had played her cards right.

Mark registered Emma's look but carefully avoided her gaze. He had the feeling that his own expression was so full of love and admiration that if he returned her glance, he'd throw her off-balance.

"You're forgetting another factor essential to the success of the unit, Emma," the chairman broke in.

She looked at him in some surprise and saw that he was now smiling broadly. "Oh?" She frowned.

"Your leadership," he replied.

"Well," Emma responded lightly, "I have to confess that that was one cost I was hoping we wouldn't have to cut."

A murmur of laughing agreement ran around the table, and the tension was momentarily relaxed.

"Well, to get to the point," Emma resumed "While we cannot safely reduce the staff-patient ratio, we don't have to use licensed staff in all areas. I suggest that we keep one fully licensed staff member in each of the therapies, and replace the others with interns. We already use psychology interns under my supervision, and with excellent results. We can also increase the ratio of attendants to registered nurses without seriously affecting the quality of treatment."

"Isn't that going to lay a considerable extra burden on your licensed staff?" The question came from an immaculately coiffed gray-haired woman leaning intently across the table from Emma.

"Mark, would you like to answer that one?" She handed the ball to him with relief. She would welcome a few minutes to prepare herself for the next question.

Mark took over smoothly.

"We discussed these proposals with the staff, Mrs. Lewis. They are all prepared to accept the additional responsibility. It's a tribute to Emma's leadership that even those staff members who will have to be replaced are willing to put the children's interests first." He looked authoritatively around the group, and when he saw no dissent continued quietly, "I am also prepared to offer supervision and individual consultation to the licensed members of the team; it would be far too much for Emma to take on alone; and they'll need some extra support. They seemed quite happy with the proposal."

"I'm sure they were, Dr. Forrest," Graves said smoothly. "But your extra time will be an additional expense, won't it?"

"I'll incorporate it into the hours I already spend on the unit," Mark replied firmly. "Emma, of course, will have rather less of my time for her own support. She's prepared, in the interests of the unit, to cut down on her consultation time."

"Is that so, Dr. Grantham?" Mrs. Lewis looked sharply at Emma, who nodded swiftly.

"I'll admit it's a sacrifice, but I don't see any alternative." She didn't add that she wasn't going to be missing out on anything; she and Mark had already agreed that if in the short term, it came down to unpaid, at-home discussion, then that was the way it had to be.

"I see," the chairman said with a quick, accepting nod, "Now what do you propose to do about the other expensive factor—unlimited length of stay?"

"That's more difficult," Emma confessed, sensing that honesty would be more effective than exaggeration. "We have two choices, as I see it. One alternative is to cut down on the number of patients we accept at any one time; but I really don't like the idea of that, because reducing our level of service doesn't look too good on statistical reports." She looked up again and noted with satisfaction the quick rumble of agreement. She'd played the right card! Everyone in the room was conscious of the need to "look good" for the politicians and the funding agencies.

"So," she went on, "we have to consider our other alternative: modifying our admissions procedure. I've revised our acceptance criteria and will leave a copy for your consideration. Third admissions will have to be abolished altogether—sad but inevitable."

"I was under the impression, Dr. Grantham, that third admissions were already against the rules." Jenner's voice broke sharply into the reflective silence that had greeted her proposals.

"You must also be aware, Dr. Jenner, that we've been making occasional exceptions to that rule. Those exceptions and our reasons for making them are well documented. I've notified you in writing on every occasion. Having received no instructions from you, I assumed that you were in favor." Emma gave a slight dismissive shrug, accepting that now she had truly burned her boats as far as Jenner was concerned. Oh, well! She'd just have to get used to the other side of the Rubicon.

"Oh, Emma! Emma!" Mark said to himself, shaking his head slightly. Why on earth had she let her tongue get the better of her at such a crucial moment? He glanced across the table. Her usually pale cheeks were pink, her eyes flashing with an annoyance that he knew was directed as much at herself as at Jenner. She gave him a look that said, Well, what did you expect me to say? His mouth curved. Everyone, after all, had a limit to his or her capacity for diplomacy—and Emma had clearly reached hers!

"Perhaps we should leave that issue for the moment." Graves's quiet voice cut the stunned atmosphere. " 'Do you have anything to add, Mark?"

Mark shook his head. "Nothing, Charles, unless there are questions?" There were plenty, and Emma, knowing that her part was now over, sat back trying to keep the angry defiance out of her face. She had transgressed the ground rules of board meeting courtesy and was furious with herself. The damage could be incalculable.

When the questions ceased, Charles Graves rose politely to escort them from the room. At the door he paused. "That wasn't very wise, Emma," he said in a low voice.

"I know. I'm sorry," she replied unhappily, casting a quick look at Mark's grim visage. "I won't hear the last of it for weeks."

Graves's eyes flicked between them, and he smiled. "In that case, Mark, I'll leave her to your tender mercies. You'll have the board's decision in a few days. Don't be too pessimistic," he added reassuringly. "You did a superb job, Emma."

Mark turned and walked out of the anteroom into the hall. Emma followed him, taking his arm. "Aren't you going to say anything?"

He looked down at her. "Well, now," he drawled, "I could point out the, um . . . lack of wisdom, shall we call it?. . . of putting down the board's appointee in front of the board. But I don't think that's necessary, do you?"

Emma shook her head. "No, it's not necessary. It was crazy, I know. But Jenner got to me just once too often. I think I'm suffering from diplomatic burnout."

Mark's hand came to rest on her shoulder, and his lips twitched. "Idiot," he chided gently. "There's a fair amount of dissatisfaction with Jenner right now. He's no longer the board's golden boy. It's just that no one, outside the confines of top administration, has ever stated a low opinion of him so openly before. You just might have done more good than harm—not that I'm condoning that particular piece of self-indulgent foolishness," he added with mock severity.

Emma frowned, feeling suddenly, inexplicably, uneasy. "If it hasn't been discussed outside top administrative circles, how do *you* know about it, Mark?" Her husband, in spite of his unfailing courtesy, was well known for his outspokenness when he thought something needed saying; however, although she knew his opinion of Jenner was as low as hers, she had never heard him articulate it in public.

"In this instance my methods are a little more devious than yours," he replied. Something in his voice stopped Emma in her tracks, and she spoke the startling thought as it flashed through her mind. "Mark, are you hoping to become Jenner's replacement?"

"It's been suggested," he responded casually—too casually.

Emma's heart seemed to find a resting place somewhere in the region of her toes as she looked at him, for the moment utterly speechless.

"How could you possibly not have told me?" she managed, eventually.

"We can't discuss this here," he said in an urgent whisper, and she became suddenly aware of the crowded hallway, the people brushing past them as they stood motionless, the curious looks directed at them.

"Where and when, then?" she asked in a low voice. "This evening, I have back-to-back sessions until six o'clock," he replied. "I'll be home by six-thirty."

"We will not discuss this at home!" They both strove to maintain a harmonious atmosphere at home, and this issue was far too big for the discussion to be kept at a well-modulated level. The last thing she wanted was for Sam, Meg, and Ted to find themselves an unwilling but involuntary audience at the first major confrontation of their marriage.

Mark took her point without further explanation.

"Come up to my office at six, then. We'll go out for dinner."

"Will you call Meg, or shall I?" This clipped dialogue dealing with the practical arrangements of their everyday life seemed curiously unreal.

"I will. I have ten minutes before my next appointment."

"We seem to be having some trouble these days sticking to our resolution to regulate our schedules," Emma said tautly. She turned on her heel and made for the elevator, not looking at him but aware of his eyes on her back as he watched her go.

Distractedly, Mark ran a weary hand through his thatch of wavy brown hair, cursing the fact that they couldn't have this out right here and now, hating the realization that she would carry that hurt and bewilderment, so clearly revealed on her face, for the rest of the afternoon. Why the hell was it impossible to foresee these things? With a deep, frustrated sigh, he turned and went off in the opposite direction.

6

" 'NIGHT, EM. See you tomorrow," the young voices chorused cheerfully as Emma made her way through the dayroom crowded with children preparing for supper. She paused at the unlocked door; she still fought the administration occasionally for the right to keep that door unlocked. For some reason, the idea of an open unit sent them into periodic convulsions. But that was just one of those petty, irritating hassles that had to be dealt with—like the extra food sent up from the main kitchen so that the kids could make snacks in their own kitchen, or even complete meals if they chose. The idea that life in a psychiatric unit should attempt to approximate the independence of home was a very scary thought for the unimaginative.

"'Night, gang. Don't do anything I wouldn't do," she responded with a supreme effort to sound her usual bright self.

"Not much chance of that!" It was Bella again. That child *never* lost an opportunity! Even through her desolation, Emma felt her face crack in a slight smile.

"You've got a lifetime ahead of you, honey," she called to the girl.

"When you leaving here, Bella?" Jerry Donovan asked, somewhat belligerently but with an underlying note of interest that set Emma's professional pulse racing.

"Dunno," was the response, as Bella became inordinately interested in a magazine lying on a table. "When Em says, I guess."

"No, Bella," Emma said quietly. "When *you* say. We don't make decisions for people around here—only suggestions."

"Lots of them," Bella muttered as an impossibly long fingernail disappeared between her teeth.

"Too many?" Emma asked. Why did this, of all evenings, have to turn into a group therapy session?

The scarlet talon broke—the crack seeming to resound in the sudden silence.

"I guess not; it just seems that way sometimes." The admission was grudging, but it was an acknowledgment nevertheless.

"Anyone else feel we make too many suggestions?" Emma looked around the room, resigning herself to a long discussion. But the children were tired—perhaps as tired as she was; a day spent trying to fit the state-mandated academic curriculum in between group and individual therapy sessions was enough to finish anyone by five-thirty.

"Anyone know what's for dinner?" The voice came from the far corner of the room and drew an immediate outburst of disgusted suggestions.

"I'll bet it's hamburger," someone groaned. "They stretch it with . . . what's that stuff called, Em?"

"Soybean," she supplied. "Enjoy! See you all in the morning."

Thankfully, she let the heavy door swing shut behind her. A lot had been said this evening that would provide meat for group discussion on another occasion, but she really wasn't up to dealing with it right now. She went up to the administrative floor. Lyn was getting ready to leave.

"Oh, Em, Mark just called. I left a message on your desk. He said his last patient canceled her appointment, so you can go on up whenever you're ready."

"Thanks, Lyn. Have a good evening." Emma smiled at the receptionist, hoping she didn't look as distracted as she felt, and went into the inner office. There was a stack of messages on her desk, but nothing that couldn't wait until morning, she decided, flicking through them quickly. She took her coat from the closet, her purse from the locked drawer in her desk, turned off the lights, locked the door to the outer office, and went miserably up to the fourth floor where the hospital consultants' offices were located.

Most people had gone home by now, and the long, institutional corridors seemed empty and desolate after the scurrying bustle of daytime. Emma hopped apologetically over a wet patch of floor, dodging the janitor's mop as he swept it across the linoleum.

Mark was tidying papers on his desk as she went in. He looked up and gave her a strained smile. "Ah, there you are. Where do you want to eat?"

"I don't care," Emma said with a slight shrug.

"That's really not too helpful, sweet," he said quietly, getting to his feet.

"I know it's not. I just can't think about anything so mundane right now. I feel totally shell-shocked." She walked numbly over to the window and gazed out into the dusk gathering over St. Anne's extensive grounds.

"Oh, dear!" He sighed heavily. "In that case, perhaps we'd better start the evening with a couple of stiff martinis. Then we'll see where we go."

"Whatever." She shrugged again.

"We'll take my car and leave the bee in the lot. You can come in with me in the morning."

"I have to be here by eight o'clock," Emma said dully.

"No problem!" She could hear the note of determined cheerfulness in his voice but could not will herself to respond.

"Let's get out of here, then." She turned toward him. "It's been a very tiring day, one way or another, and I've had enough of this building."

Mark resisted the urge to take her in his arms, to kiss the fatigue from her eyes, to stroke the tension from her taut, slender body. Later, when they had sorted out the mess that, however unwittingly, he had created, she would accept his offer of comfort and reassurance, but not now. He walked to the door, held it for her, and she went past him into the corridor.

A shiver ran through Emma as she brushed against him, a longing to hurl herself against the broad chest, to be patted and comforted and told that everything was going to be all right, that life was going to be as it had been. But it could never again be as it had been. Mark had revealed something about himself that she had never guessed—that his ambitions lay in the direction of top administration, that he was not utterly, and to the exclusion of all else, dedicated to front-line work. Even if he didn't take Jenner's job, there would be others. He was far too ambitious and self-driven to accept anything less than his ultimate aim. She just hadn't realized how different their individual goals were!

They drove in silence, enclosed in the purring warmth of the BMW, out of the suburbs and toward the city.

"Do you mind if we go to the Sheraton?" Mark broke the quiet. "We won't have a parking problem, and we can drink and eat there."

"Not at all," she acquiesced, trying to sound as if it was a matter of any interest. Apparently, she didn't succeed, for he sighed again, and then silence hung heavily over them once more.

The bar at the Sheraton was not at all quiet—in fact, it seethed with excited participants at various conventions—but, in a way, Emma thought, that was better. At least if they were going to quarrel, they could do so without being conspicuous.

Their drinks arrived, and Mark looked at her carefully.

"Perhaps you should start, Emma."

"Why me?" With the blue swizzle stick, she poked at the olive in the clear liquid. "You're the one who's supposed to explain."

"I'll answer you," he said quietly.

"That puts all the burden on me. I'm not going to sit here and be analyzed, Mark! You put this joker on the table; you put it back in the pack." She was angry now, with an anger that grew from her deep, confused hurt.

"I don't *have* anything to say, darling. Charles Graves approached me early last week and asked me informally if, in principle, I would be interested. It hasn't gone any further than that."

"And you didn't consider mentioning this to me?"

"Not until I had decided whether I *was* interested," he responded. "I couldn't see any point in getting into an intense discussion over something that wasn't going to happen."

"Just as you didn't see any point in mentioning the prospect of budget cuts until they'd happened." She couldn't keep the bitterness out of her voice.

"That was a mistake," he admitted flatly. "I was trying to save you what could have been unnecessary worrying. But things moved a lot faster than I'd expected, and we were both caught unawares."

"All right, I accept that. But this is different. You've never given me so much as a hint that you have political ambitions."

"Hardly political."

"Oh, yes, Mark! Totally political! Running a hospital the size of St. Anne's is going to be all wheeling and dealing."

She drained her glass, and Mark instantly raised a finger in the direction of the waiter.

"Is that what's bothering you?"

"I feel betrayed," she said with a sudden sigh of defeat. "I thought we shared the same goals, the same values. You never gave me so much as an inkling that we don't."

"We do."

"We *don't!*" she denied emphatically. "Not if you want to spend the rest of your life pushing paper for a large salary instead of concerning yourself with the people who make that paperwork necessary."

"I fail to see why the two things should be mutually exclusive." Mark was angry now. She could see it in the sudden tautness of his lips, the hardening of his usually warm brown eyes, the rigidity of his broad shoulders. But her own anger rose to meet his. She took an overlong sip of her fresh martini.

"You'll have no time to be a psychiatrist. You know that as well as I do. You'll just be a bureaucrat. What about your practice? What's going to happen to that?" She gulped down the rest of her drink; then, with a quick shake of her head, signaled the waiter.

"I don't think another martini is going to do you much good," Mark observed quietly.

"I'll be the judge of that! It can't make me feel any worse than I do already." She chewed her lip miserably for a minute. "Well, aren't you going to answer my question? What about your practice?"

"I won't have time for it as you've just pointed out."

"And the kids' unit? I thought you were going to become *more* involved there, not less."

"I was hoping we could discuss alternatives in a constructive fashion," he said tightly.

"What alternatives are there?" Emma demanded.

"Another consultant, or preferably another psychiatrist assigned on a full-time basis. It's far too heavy a load for you, even with my help."

"No!" she exclaimed in horror. "I can't work with anyone else. I could never trust anyone the way I do you. Most people aren't as flexible as we are."

"Aren't you making just a few too many generalizations?" Mark asked levelly. "There *are* other psychiatrists."

"Why are you attacking me?" What on earth was happening to them? They had never quarreled like this before. She had never even imagined that they could. They were supposed to like and respect each other far too much. But now there was nothing between them but anger; and Emma felt an overpowering sense of betrayal that seemed to prick her in a thousand tiny stabs until her skin felt raw, every nerve exposed.

"I don't want to attack you, but you're shooting arrows in my direction so fast that I don't have time to defend myself," Mark snapped, then sighed. "Look, love, can we just try to take hold of ourselves before one of us says something we're both going to regret?"

Emma ignored his plea. "You realize, don't you, that if you take Jenner's job you'll technically be my boss?"

"Not just technically," he responded swiftly, and she felt the color drain from her cheeks.

"What's that going to do to *us?*"

"I don't see why it should do anything at all."

"Don't be so naive! I'm always having some sort of

battle with the administration, as well you know. And from now on, I'll be battling with *you*." Suddenly, the full, horrendous impact of the situation hit her.

"It's always possible that, since I understand a great deal more about the unit than previous medical directors, you won't need to battle." He spoke quietly, with a visible effort at reasonableness.

"The unit breaks bureaucratic rules because it has to. It's not the particular individual I fight; it's what the individual represents." Emma's voice was a dull monotone now. "I can't imagine that our personal relationship won't be affected when I'm constantly having to defend my actions to you at work. You've always fought on my side before." Her statement died on a note of defeat, and she pushed back her chair abruptly. "I'm sorry. I have to leave. I can't take any more of this right now. I'll grab a taxi in front of the hotel."

Mark made no attempt to stop her as she walked swiftly out of the crowded bar. He sat for a long time looking into his glass. Emma was right to a large extent, but surely they had enough common ground to work out a compromise? He went in search of a solitary, tasteless, but necessary dinner before collecting the car from the underground garage and making his desolate way home. It was going to be a long night, but this mess had to be resolved before they went to bed.

The house was quiet as he let himself in, but Meg appeared instantly at the kitchen door as if she'd been listening for him.

"Where's Emma?" he asked, giving her a somewhat strained smile of greeting.

"In bed, I think. She came in around eight and went straight upstairs." Meg moved back into the kitchen and he followed her.

"Did I keep you up?"

"No, of course not. Ted and I were just having a nightcap. Do you want some hot chocolate? I can heat up some more milk."

"No, thanks, Meg. Did Emma eat anything?" He waved a hand in greeting toward Ted, who was firmly ensconced in the rocker by the stove.

"Not as far as I know," Meg replied. "What's going on, Mark?"

Mark shook his head wearily. "It's too long a story for tonight, Meg, and it's not over yet. Do we have any canned soup?"

"There's some lobster bisque in the cupboard," Meg replied easily. "Em's favorite."

"That's fortunate," he said dryly. "My chances of getting anything down her tonight that's not her favorite are about zero!"

"That bad, eh?" Ted murmured.

"That bad!" Mark opened the can, poured the contents into a saucepan, set it on the stove, and stood watching it restlessly.

"You sure there's nothing we can do?" Meg asked anxiously.

"Quite sure, thanks. I'm sorry about this; it wreaks havoc with the happy family atmosphere." He laughed mirthlessly.

Ted got to his feet with a shrug and a yawn. "Meg and I aren't always the most peaceable pair." He grinned at his wife. "However, before that infant daughter of ours decides prematurely that it's morning, I'd like to get some sleep."

"Only sleep? You disappoint me!" Meg laughed and followed him downstairs to their large basement apartment.

The soup bubbled at last, and with a heavy but resolute heart, Mark filled a bowl, set it on a tray with a plate of crackers, and went upstairs.

Emma was sitting up in bed reading, and he had a sudden absurd urge to laugh. She was wearing one of his shirts buttoned to the neck, the sheet was pulled up to her shoulders, and her face was hidden behind her glasses and the corn-silk cascade of her hair. He had never before seen her produce such a blatant picture of well-defended vulnerability,

She looked up at him through the waterfall of hair and mumbled a greeting, trying to control the turbulent emotions that surged up in her at the sight of Mark, whose stance and expression showed every sign that he was about to become bossy again.

He set the tray on the dresser and walked carefully over to the bed. "First, I think we'll get rid of the armor, Emma mine."

"Leave me alone," she protested feebly as he removed her glasses, putting them carefully on the night table. He didn't reply, merely tossed her hair over her shoulders and lifted her face. Her eyes were red, and there were dark smudges in the hollows beneath them.

"My poor sweet," he whispered, bending to kiss the hot, swollen eyelids. "Let me take away the pain."

"You can't," she said on a soft note of despair.

"I can, if you'll let me." He began to unbutton the shirt.

"No!" Emma fought his hands. "I want to keep it on."

"It's coming off," Mark said firmly, "and then you're going to eat your soup." The last button came undone; he took a firm grip on one wrist of the shirt and pulled, then did the same with the other one. Emma dragged the sheet up to her throat in a convulsive, protective movement.

Mark set the tray on her knees. "I'm not hungry," she groaned.

"Sweet, you haven't had a thing since lunchtime except three very dry martinis," he responded calmly. "If you had any lunch, that is."

She couldn't disguise the quick, conscious flash in her eyes. She had been far too keyed up about the board meeting to eat lunch.

"Exactly!" he said with a certain grim satisfaction, and went into the bathroom. When he returned in his bathrobe some ten minutes later, the bowl and plate were empty.

"More?" He raised an eyebrow, bending to take the tray.

"Is there more?"

"The rest of the can's on the stove. I'll go get it." Emma sat back against the pillows. She was—miraculously and for no apparent reason, unless it was the soup—beginning to feel better. They hadn't resolved anything yet, but she had nothing left to say. She had cried herself to a standstill in the last couple of hours and was now drained, empty, waiting for Mark to put the jumbled jigsaw puzzle back together again. He looked as exhausted and miserable as she did, but there was a certain grim resolve beneath the weary exterior that was curiously, ineffably, reassuring. He wasn't about to leave them both wallowing in the mud of their mutual hurt and anger. She wasn't, either, but his reserves of strength seemed greater than hers tonight. She had used hers all up in the board meeting and over that disastrous, three-martini shouting match in the Sheraton, during which, she admitted to herself ruefully, she had been doing most of the shouting. Now she would listen. They were both adults, after all; they had found each other after years of individual maturation and had had their own pains and joys during those earlier years. Marriage was, in the final analysis, a reciprocal relationship involving two totally separate individuals. The had to work on their relationship every minute they were together, and the base of the marriage would constantly shift as their inevitable separateness produced kaleidoscopic changes that, if dealt with properly, would only enrich it.

Mark reappeared with a tray that bore two steaming mugs and another bowl of soup. He gave her a searching, frowning look and seemed to read in her face her thoughts of the last few minutes. He smiled slowly, almost tentatively, and her heart went out to him.

"I don't want to fight anymore, love," she murmured, managing to produce a very shaky smile of her own.

"I don't think we ever did, did we?" He sat down on the edge of the bed, placing the tray carefully beside him.

"What have you got there?" Emma leaned over, inhaling deeply of the rich aroma issuing from the mugs.

"Eggnog," he replied. "Something bland and soothing seemed in order."

"I guess," she agreed, attacking her soup hungrily.

He waited until she had finished before laying a large hand, palm up, beside the tray in undemanding invitation. She gave him her own, and the firm squeeze he gave it sent strong waves of reassurance through every overworked nerve of her body.

"How could we ever have allowed such an appalling thing to happen to us?" she whispered on a deep sigh.

"We did. It did." Mark's lips curved in a wan attempt at a smile. "And I don't suppose, my darling, that it'll be the last time."

"No," she concurred softly. "I don't suppose it will. You really want to be medical director of St. Anne's?"

"Not if you tell me you couldn't stand it." Those brown eyes held hers, telling her that he spoke the truth.

"I couldn't do that." Emma's smile was a replica of his. "Your life is your own. I couldn't live with myself if I prevented your doing something that's absolutely necessary for you."

"But I couldn't live with myself if I did something that was anathema to you."

"But you *do* want it?" she persisted.

"I want it, but our marriage is my first priority," he replied simply.

"*Anathema* is a big word," Emma said quietly. "I don't *like* the idea of your becoming an administrator, as I rather suspect you've gathered." He laughed, and for the first time all day, some of the intensity left them both. "That doesn't mean I can't live with it, though," she continued, sipping the rich, creamy liquid in her mug. Suddenly, she grinned.

"Actually, Mark Forrest, you'll be very good at administration! It'll give you an outlet for this alarming predilection toward bossiness that you're beginning to display."

"Reckon it'll let you off the hook, do you?" he growled, reaching for her mug.

"You'll never unhook me, Dr. Forrest. Ow!" she squealed, making an ineffectual grab for the covers as he pulled them off.

"Now what are you going to do, little-fish-on-the-end-of-my-line?" He grinned wickedly, devouring her soft, naked vulnerability with his eyes.

"What do little caught fish usually do?" She grinned back.

"They jerk and they dance and they wriggle. Will you do the same, my pretty little goldfish?" His eyes glowed like hot coals, warming her to her core.

"Depends how you play your line," she murmured, dropping her eyelashes demurely.

"Oh, Emma mine! How can you do this to me? I've never wanted to possess any one or anything the way I do you. I want every inch of you to know that you are possessed." He was still touching her only with his eyes, and the hot center of her being was spreading in waves of molten gold to every extremity of her body.

"We're both possessed, my own." Her arms reached for him, pulled him down hard against her as she undid the belt of his robe, pushed the silky material away so that his skin was seared with her own. Mark groaned against the hollow of her neck, his lips nuzzling the soft flesh before his teeth nipped gently but insistently—as if he needed, in some way, to brand her. Her hands slipped beneath his robe, ran over the hard-muscled back, gripped the taut buttocks in a convulsive frenzy of ecstatic anticipation as he raised his body and drove deep into her center. His mouth was now on hers in a deep, fierce, possessive kiss that she matched, urgent thrust for urgent thrust, and as the hot metal of their separateness fused in an electric, sparking shower, her nails dug into his hips, marking him as her own.

"No, hold me," she whispered insistently as she felt him begin to move out of her. Mark rolled onto his side, wrapping her in his arms so that they remained joined as they lay breathlessly trying to recapture reality.

"I love you, Mr. Medical Director," Emma murmured, the instant before she slipped, in the still-lighted room, over the edge into the black sleep of utter emotional exhaustion.

She awoke a few hours later in complete darkness. Her body was making fairly insistent demands, and with a soft moan of protest she started to crawl out of bed. Mark was fast asleep, lying on his stomach, one arm curled heavily around her waist. As she moved away, he mumbled incoherently, tightened his hold, followed her body with his.

"Let me go idiot," she said, laughing gently, as she lifted the imprisoning arm from her waist.

"Where are you going?" he mumbled.

"To the bathroom! You can't expect to fill me full of martinis and soup and eggnog and then expect me to last the night!"

"Guess not," he grumbled, "but hurry up; it's lonely!"

She returned within minutes, stumbling across the dark room, diving under the covers to curl against him. Strong arms went around her, lifted her on top of him. "Hey," she expostulated with a chuckle, "you're supposed to be asleep." He didn't feel asleep!

"I am, but there are some things I can do in my sleep."

"You are utterly inexhaustible, husband," she whispered, adjusting her position to accommodate him. "But tomorrow's only Wednesday."

"Today is Wednesday," he corrected, "but I don't think this is going to work."

"Whatever do you mean?" She collapsed in a fit of sleepy giggles against his chest.

"Well, I don't have the energy to move up, and you don't have the energy to move down, and nothing is going to happen in a state of inertia!"

A firm hand at the small of her back, another in the hollow behind her knee, and he rolled them both onto their sides, pulling her leg across his hip. "Ah . . ." he sighed in utter contentment, "that's *much* better." The slow drowsy rhythm established itself, swept in a soft, honeyed tide of peaceful warmth over them and through them. No cataclysmic finale this time, no need to demand ownership, no need for anything; they were at peace, body with body, mind with mind, for this moment joined in blissful union.

"Come in, Emma. Please sit down." Charles Graves, with the New England courtesy for which he was known, helped her into an armchair at one end of his large office and sat down facing her. "I'm sorry we've kept you hanging so long." He smiled. "I promised you a decision within a few days, and it's actually been three weeks, but there was some opposition to deal with."

Emma's heart leaped. Was he implying that the opposition *had* been dealt with? Nothing showed in her face, however, as she said quietly, "I don't suppose my outburst helped matters?"

He considered her thoughtfully. "Well, it certainly produced complications. Without that, you would have won your case immediately. As it was"—he paused, and a slight smile touched his lips"—you opened a can of worms. I rather think that was what you intended, Emma." His eyes narrowed speculatively.

"I didn't intend to open it right then," she confessed frankly.

"Well, no matter." He shrugged lightly. "As far as the kids' unit is concerned, you have carte blanche to make your modifications—within the budget constraints, of course."

"Of course," she agreed smoothly and then allowed her face to register her pleasure. There didn't seem any point in hiding it from Charles Graves. "Thank you, Charles," she said warmly.

"Don't thank me, Emma." He leaned over and patted her hand. "Your commitment to those children convinced everyone."

"Except Jenner," she couldn't help saying.

The chairman fixed her with a steady eye. "You won't have to worry about Dr. Jenner much longer."

Emma didn't pretend not to know what he meant. "How soon?" she asked.

"His resignation is on my desk. Mark will be offered the position formally this afternoon, to take effect when he gets back from the convention in London at the end of April."

"Well, at least the suspense won't be prolonged," Emma said levelly, but she felt her stomach muscles knot. Mark's appointment was only six weeks away!

"Are you really against it, Emma?"

"No, absolutely not!" she said quickly and genuinely. "I was, initially, but it's right for Mark, and I couldn't stand in his way."

"Of course not," Graves concurred somberly. "But I'd hate it to cause trouble between you."

"It's not going to be clear sailing." Emma laughed ruefully. "Nevertheless, we'll manage."

He looked at her seriously. "You know, Mark will be very good for St. Anne's."

"Yes, he will," Emma declared firmly. "This institution needs a maverick, but an objective, diplomatic one—that's Mark."

"It is, and it could be you, if you weren't so utterly and necessarily bound up with the kids' unit." Charles got to his feet, holding out a courteous helping hand as she rose. "I understand, Emma, that in the interests of the children you have to negotiate continually with the administration. No one here has a free hand; we all have to abide by the rules and regulations of our financial masters. Mark isn't going to impose those rules on you and the unit unnecessarily."

"I know that, Charles." She smiled tremulously. "It's just that bureaucracies are so self-serving, and there's so little room for individuality."

"*You* don't do too badly, Dr. Grantham," he replied, chuckling as he walked her to the door. "I haven't noticed you compromising your individuality much!"

"I haven't had to yet—but only because I'm giving the hospital something it needs politically," she came back with swift candor.

"I can hardly argue with you," he said with a resigned shrug. "But you and Mark make a fine team, and you both have the absolute confidence of the board." He smiled suddenly, laying an avuncular arm over her shoulders. "In fact, we're actually appointing both of you, as a team. Your inside knowledge of the workings of this hospital will be invaluable for the new medical director, and I can't believe he won't listen to you."

"He'd better!" She grinned.

The cork on the Möet et Chandon exploded just as Mark walked into the kitchen that evening. His face split into a wide, beaming grin as a well-prepared Sam yelled, an instant before everyone else, "C'gratulations!"

"What a welcome!" He scooped up the excited little boy, buried his mouth for a moment against the soft, round cheek, held the small, shining head tightly.

"I'ss a s'prise party," Sam burbled. "We got Doritos 'n' ginger ale."

"What a lucky pair we are." Mark laughed softly, looking across at Emma. She smiled, encompassing them both with all the love she had to give, as if her life depended on it.

"Some of us can have a little champagne, too." She filled the crystal glasses with an amazingly steady hand, passing them out to a smiling Ted and Meg. "Congratulations, darling." She stood on tiptoe to kiss him, her eyes saying everything she would say later when they were alone.

"It's truly all right?" He whispered the soft question against her lips.

"Truly," she whispered back, and meant it. This was no time for reservations or apprehensions. Mark was her husband, her lover and best friend, and she vowed that his joys would be her joys, his celebration her own.

7

"COME HERE, LITTLE BUNDLE." Mark pulled her warm, languid body toward him in the bed as he spoke the soft, sleepy words.

"Bundle of what," Emma mumbled dopily, snuggling against him.

"All kinds of delicious things!" His low chuckle rustled through her hair as he began to touch her in the way that only he knew, awakening her drowsy senses, and bringing every nerve ending to life.

"I do love Saturday mornings," Emma purred, stretching catlike beneath the covers, raising her body to the glorious strokes.

The bedroom door crashed open suddenly, and a small, pajamaed ball landed heavily on top of them. "Mornin'" Sam shrilled gleefully, tugging at the covers. "I'ss Satday!"

Emma groaned as Mark struggled into a sitting position. "Sam," he said carefully, "it's quite possible that there's something the matter with my ears, but I didn't hear you knock."

The child chewed his lip, wrinkling his small, pert nose. "Forgot," he muttered.

"Well, in that case, Sam Richards, I think we'd better start the day again, don't you?" Mark swung him off the bed and set him down firmly on the floor. The little boy looked at him for a moment, his thought processes so clearly revealed on his face that Emma was hard put not to laugh. Mark regarded the child steadily, and Sam, who had known his stepfather for two of his three-and-a-half years, finally turned and stomped out of the room, closing the door with a protesting bang.

"It's very hard for him," Emma said with a slight smile. "He's used to treating my bedroom as if it's his, and it's only in the last three months that things have changed."

"Maybe so," Mark grumbled, "but it's not good for my psychological or physical well-being to be interrupted at such a delicate moment!"

She laughed. "We have to remember to lock the door."

"If Sam would remember to knock, I wouldn't have to remember to lock the door."

"Well, since he'll probably be back once he's recovered his good nature, I suppose there's no point picking up where we left off?" Emma sighed.

"Maybe we can persuade him to take a little nap this afternoon." Mark grinned.

"On a Saturday? Fat chance! It's his day with us, and he's not going to miss a minute of it."

There was a loud, exaggerated thump on the door, and they called in unison, "Good morning, Sam."

Mark held out his arms to the small figure standing on the threshold, clutching a mangled teddy bear by one mangy foot. "Think you can make it in one?" He smiled.

Sam measured the distance with a considering frown and then beamed as he took a flying leap across the floor and into Mark's inviting arms. Emma pulled back the covers, and the child, with a deft wriggle, inserted himself and the bear between them. A well-sucked thumb went into his mouth accompanied by a contented sigh, and for a while there was quiet.

"When's Daddy comin' back from Pewu?" Sam's question jerked Emma out of a delicious half-doze.

"Hard to say exactly, darling. He said in his last letter that he was hoping to be back next week."

"I goin' to New York to stay wiv him?"

"You're going in April, when Mark and I go to London, but I'm sure it'll be fine with Daddy if you want to go before. Would you like to?" She propped herself up on one elbow, smiling down at him.

"Dunno," he said casually.

Her eyes met Mark's, and she raised her eyebrows questioningly. Did he think there was any more to the exchange than there seemed to be? He understood her question, but his slight shrug told her that he didn't know, either.

"I'm going to make some tea," he announced. "Sam, you want to come down, too, and bring up the paper for Mommy?"

"Yus," Sam asserted, clambering out of the warm nest.

"It's your turn to do the shopping this weekend, isn't it, Mark?" Meg looked across the kitchen table.

"For my sins," he groaned. "Is that the list?" He held out a hand across the breakfast jumble of plates and cups.

"It's rather long, I'm afraid."

Mark looked at it. "Long!" he exclaimed incredulously. "The only thing that's missing here is the kitchen sink, Meg!"

"Well, Emma wasn't able to get everything last Saturday," Meg explained.

"Traitor!" Emma accused, making a strategic dash for the kitchen door.

"Not so fast!" Mark's hand shot out at the speed of light

and snagged her wrist. He pulled her down with a thump onto his knee. "Explain!"

She sighed. "The supermarket was like a scene by Hieronymus Bosch. Everyone was going the wrong way up the aisles . . ."

"You, of course, were the only one out of several hundred people going the right way?" he interrupted with a rumble of laughter.

"I always am," she replied with dignity. "But it wasn't just that: The checkout lines could have circled the earth! I got so fed up, I just bought the essentials."

"Assuming that your mild-tempered, complacent husband would trot off obediently the next week and do double duty without question?" he demanded severely.

"I wouldn't put it *quite* like that." Her eyes danced as laughter threatened to get the better of her.

"Well, *I* would," he asserted unequivocally. "I think, in all fairness, Emma mine, that you're going to have to come with me this morning."

"Oh, Mark, that means I'll have gone three weeks in a row," she complained. "And besides, we always quarrel when we go shopping together. You're too slow!"

"I'm merely careful about the order in which I put things into the cart," he objected. "You throw everything in as you see what you need, and then end up at the checkout with a large can of tomato purée, a dozen bruised peaches, shapeless bread, and a dozen leaky containers of yogurts at the bottom!"

Everyone was laughing now, and baby Anna banged her spoon on the tray of her high chair in vigorous contribution.

"Okay," Emma groaned resignedly. "If I must, I must."

"I come too," Sam stated in a spray of toast crumbs.

"Oh, no!" they both moaned. Grocery shopping with Sam turned an already horrendous expedition into a total nightmare. But weekends were his time.

"May as well be hanged for a sheep as a lamb," Emma said wryly. "A family trip it will be."

"With one deviation from the norm," Mark announced, still holding her firmly on his knee.

"Oh . . . ?" She raised her eyebrows quizzically.

"This particular family generally suffers from a surfeit of generals and a deficit of privates! Today, there's going to be only one general—me!"

"You're outrageous!" She laughed, burying her head in his shoulder. "On one condition, then."

"No conditions! This is absolutely non-negotiable," he declared, trying to control his own merriment.

"One condition! The privates get a hot fudge sundae afterward."

"The only thing I'm promising you, Emma mine, is instant retribution if you step out of line," he stated, tipping her off his knee as he got to his feet. "I'm going to shave. This expedition will leave at nine A.M. sharp! If you two aren't ready, you'll come as you are." He looked meaning-fully at Emma's skimpy nightgown, which barely reached her knees.

"Mark's funny." Sam beamed milkily around the room as the door closed behind Mark.

"He certainly thinks he is," Emma replied, gathering up dirty dishes and beginning to load the dishwasher.

"I'll do that." Meg grinned. "I'd hate to see you eating a

hot fudge sundae in your P.J.'s! It's a bit chilly out there."

Emma looked at her image in the glass that evening and nodded complacently. The beaded Chinese collar of the turquoise satin evening dress showed off her long, creamy neck; the material flowed over her unrestrained breasts, clung to her waist, curved over her hips as if it had been made on her—as, indeed, it almost had, she reflected with a smile. She heard Mark calling good night to Sam and turned quickly toward the door.

"Do you think he's ever going to get tired of that story about the dragon?" he asked and then stopped, eyes widening. "Wow! Another of Jacqueline's creations?"

"Mmm. Like it?" She turned slowly. His expression in the mirror was all she had hoped it would be.

"You outrageous sorceress!" he exclaimed, striding across the room. "How dare you?"

"There's nothing wrong with it," she insisted, her eyes gleaming with merriment. "It's only my back."

"Only!" He ran a warm, flat palm down the length of her bare back. "A quarter-inch lower, and you'd be showing the world what's for my eyes only!" He slipped a finger under the tight waistband of the skirt to demonstrate his point. Emma shivered at his touch.

"Are you going to play the outraged husband?" she asked mischievously.

His eyes narrowed, began to glow with the sensual promise that always sent quivers of excitement trembling through her.

"No . . . no, I don't think so," he said thoughtfully. "But I think we might make one minor adjustment."

"Oh?" Then she gasped as he began to lift the long silky skirt, drawing it up her legs to her waist. "Mark, stop it!" she exclaimed softly. "We don't have time, and I'll get all creased."

"Take them off," he murmured against her ear, his eyes riveting hers in the mirror.

"Are you serious?" she asked incredulously.

"Do it!" he whispered urgently, nipping her earlobe insistently.

She wriggled out of her pantyhose and felt the satin skirt slide back again, cool and soft over her bare skin, to fall to her ankles.

Mark gave her a smile of pure deviltry in the mirror as he ran his hands over her thighs, her bottom, feeling the naked flesh beneath the skirt. "I suspect that this very private little joke is going to enliven an otherwise rather dull evening," he said softly. "Every time I look at you, you're going to know exactly what I'm thinking."

"I'll never get through the evening," she whispered, as waves of desire flooded her. "You really expect me to sit, quite naked under this ridiculous dress, amid that formal, stuffy crowd and keep a straight face?"

"I do." He nodded firmly. "You shouldn't wear clothes that give me wicked ideas!"

"But you're giving the keynote address," she protested as laughter shook in her voice. They were attending the annual dinner of the Psychiatrists' Association, in which Mark played a very active part. His prospective appointment as medical director of St. Anne's had made him the inevitable choice to address the meeting, and Emma had already realized that she was a lot more nervous than he seemed to be. But she hadn't realized *quite* how insouciant he clearly was.

"It'll add a little spice to the task." He grinned. "Just keep your eyes on your plate."

An hour later, as they walked into the ballroom of the Hyatt Regency in Cambridge, Mark laid a warm hand possessively on the hollow of her back, and Emma glanced up at him. He smiled and dropped one eyelid in an impish wink.

"I like being married to you," she murmured. "You're more fun than a barrelful of monkeys."

"You ain't seen nothin' yet, kid," he replied with a grin, and then they were caught up in the throng and went their separate ways.

It was a scene familiar to them both, and Emma, in spite of her dislike of formality, began to enjoy herself. She knew most of the people present, and many of them were good friends. She found herself sitting at dinner between two of her favorite colleagues, and was in the middle of an animated, friendly argument when she felt her skin prickle. She looked across the table. Mark, at the far end, was fixing her with a steady gaze, his eyes dancing down the table. She stammered to a halt, and her cheeks warmed as all coherent thought left her. She felt totally naked and knew that Mark was telling her that, for him, she was. She shook her head furiously, and his lips twitched as he turned courteously to answer his neighbor.

For the rest of the meal, she kept her eyes firmly on her plate and her attention on her dinner companions. It didn't help too much, since she didn't need her eyes to tell her when Mark was looking at her.

"Ladies and gentlemen, we are fortunate that our well-known colleague, Dr. Mark Forrest, has agreed to address us this evening." The association's chairman called the chattering throng to order, and Emma looked toward the podium. Her husband was standing, utterly relaxed, beside the chairman, and the certainty flashed through her mind that one day, in the not too distant future, Mark would head this large, powerful group. Would her heart ever cease to somersault when she looked at him? she wondered distractedly. It really didn't seem to matter what he wore, but, tonight, he looked particularly elegant. The superb cut of his dinner jacket molded his broad, strong physique, and the crisp white ruffles of his dress shirt set off his normally tanned complexion, the deep brown humorous eyes, the wavy brown hair that was always just a little longer than his male colleagues'.

He thanked the chairman for his introduction, stepped to the podium, looked directly at her. Emma deliberately moistened her lips with the tip of her tongue, dropped her eyelashes, and shifted seductively on her chair. Mark's face broke into that broad, devastating smile that would cause every female heart in the room to skip a beat. Emma instantly dropped her gaze. It really wasn't fair to torment him at this juncture, even though he'd been teasing her similarly all evening.

As he began to speak, he soon had the audience in the palm of his hand. He was addressing the question of therapeutic accountability, a thorny subject much on everyone's minds at the moment, and was doing it superbly. Emma knew the speech by heart, had lived with it for weeks, but it sounded quite different now as Mark's deep, mellow tones rang with quiet authority around the room. He made them laugh, too, throwing in apposite jokes that had not been in his original script. He wasn't even looking at his notes; his hands rested, broad, square, calm, on the lectern.

"That husband of yours really speaks well," Craig Grant, her neighbor, whispered in her ear.

"He does everything well." She smiled, fascinated by the sense of proprietorial pride washing through her. Applause rang through the room and, with a warm smile of thanks that seemed to encompass his entire audience, Mark crossed the room toward her.

"Just wait till I get you home, Emma Grantham!" he warned in a low murmur, bending over her shoulder.

"Why? What did I do?" she asked with mock innocence, turning to face him.

"You know damn well! Looking at me like that! I completely forgot what I was about to say!"

"You recovered quickly enough." Her lips brushed his lightly, in congratulation.

"Come dance," he demanded, pulling back her chair.

"Newlyweds." Craig chuckled. "Just wait! Give yourselves a year or so and the last person you'll want to dance with is each other."

"Never!" Emma declared firmly, following Mark with a quick skip as he tugged her behind him onto the dance floor.

"Never!" he echoed, pulling her close.

"Mark, you're dancing to the wrong tune," she informed him as the loud, frenetic beat pounded around them and he persisted in moving as if it were a slow waltz, his hands running seductively over her back and for one breathless instant cupping her buttocks. The touch seemed to burn through the dress to her bare skin beneath.

"I've never been able to understand this passion for gyrating around six feet away from one's partner," he grumbled. "It's like trying to make love from opposite sides of the room."

"Speaking of which . . ." she murmured, fluttering her eyelashes.

His eyes darkened. "Good grief, I have to get that dress off you! Come on, you sexy little bundle of enchantment, we're going home." He, seized her hands and practically hauled her off the polished oval dance floor.

"Oh, Mark, I was looking for you." The chairman of the association shouldered his way toward them, interrupting their somewhat hasty retreat. Mark sighed, and his grip on Emma's wrist slackened.

"I need a few minutes of your time," the chairman continued. "Just a couple of points I want to clarify for the next meeting. You don't mind, Emma?" He flashed a perfunctory smile in her general direction.

She said aloud, "No, no, of course not, Peter," but she thought, Yes, I *do* mind. Resignedly, she started to withdraw her wrist from Mark's hand, and was astonished when his fingers tightened. He was a politician, and politicians did what they had to; if Peter was asking for a chat, surely Mark had to acquiesce?

But Mark was saying, "I'm terribly sorry, Peter, but I'll have to call you tomorrow. I seem to have eaten something that's disagreed with me, and I really can't stop now!" With a charming but unmistakably dismissive smile, he strode rapidly toward the door, with Emma half-running in his wake, fighting the giggles that threatened to overtake her before they reached the sanctuary of the foyer. Once there, she collapsed against him, and they clung to each other as paroxysms of hilarity swept through them.

"Oh, Mark, how could you have said such a thing?" she gasped. "Did you see Peter's face?"

"I wasn't looking," he choked, "but everyone's gaping at us right now. Perhaps we should take a room here?"

"Be serious for a minute, Mark."

"I am," Mark announced firmly. "That's exactly what we're going to do."

"But they don't rent them by the hour," she protested weakly, following willy-nilly as he tugged her toward the registration desk.

"Who said anything about renting by the hour?" he demanded with a low growl. "I'm having you for a *very* long night."

The well-trained desk clerk didn't bat an eye as she handed Mark a room key. Emma didn't know whether her cheeks were scarlet with embarrassment, suppressed mirth, or sheer excitement.

Mark flicked on the light switches in the comfortable room that looked like any other in any similar hotel and, pulling her with him, sat down in the armchair, drawing her between his knees.

"At last," he muttered with a sigh of relief and began to explore her body through the dress. His hands lingered over her breasts, which swelled softly beneath the satin; a hard fingertip rubbed insistently until her nipples peaked, taut and wanting against the sensuous material. He murmured with satisfaction and moved slowly downward, feeling with a firm thumb for the sharp points of her hip-bones as his palm flattened over her belly. Emma trembled as the glowing embers of passion flared into bright life, and Mark smiled contentedly.

"How I love to do this to you, Emma mine," he whispered. "I only have to touch you in the ways I know and you quiver for me." His hands moved down her thighs, slipped up to her buttocks and squeezed their hard round-ness; she arched her back in almost desperate, involuntary response. She couldn't deny his statement, even if she had wanted to. She also knew that this was going to be one of Mark's marathons. He'd promised a long night, and he never broke his promises!

Suddenly, he parted his knees, removing the imprisoning pressure, and gently pushed her away from him. "Take the dress off," he commanded huskily, leaning back in the chair. His eyes were hooded but demanding.

Slowly, she began to undo the tiny buttons at the neck of the dress. Jacqueline had a passion for a myriad of tiny but-tons, and while they were very pretty, they were most inconvenient at times! Her fingers fumbled, her excitement making her movements awkward, but Mark made no attempt to help her, merely linked his hands behind his head, his relaxed posture totally belied by the smoldering glow in his eyes. At last, the final button opened, and very, very slowly she slipped the dress off one shoulder, holding a hand to her breast to prevent the bodice from slipping any farther than she wished. Mark's eyes narrowed as she changed hands and bared the other shoulder. She cupped the material to her breasts with both hands and looked steadily at him.

"Let go," he instructed softly.

"Take off your jacket," she returned quietly.

His lips curved as he saw her game, and he complied hastily, dropping the jacket to the floor before resuming his relaxed position.

She revealed her breasts by tantalizing degrees, the soft, creamy mounds crowned with their hard, pink tips. Then she held the dress firmly to her waist.

His tongue touched his lips as he inhaled sharply. "Farther, Emma mine."

She shook her head. "Take off your shirt."

It was his turn now to fumble with the tiny studs in his dress shirt, the awkward links in the cuffs, and she stood still, watching his struggles in the way he'd watched hers. But at last the shirt joined the jacket.

"Turn around very slowly as you slide the dress down." She obeyed the throbbing directive, her breath catching as she revolved with infinite deliberation, pushing the material over her hips until it fell in a turquoise cascade around her ankles.

"I have an advantage over you." His low chuckle filled the room. "You have no more cards to play, my sweet Emma."

She turned back to face him, saw the mischief in his eyes, and laughed acquiescently. "I made the most of what I had."

"Indeed you did! Come here now. I want to play with you." He reached for her, pulling her back between his knees, and she smiled tremulously, her skin prickling, pulses racing, as she felt the silky texture of his trousers against her naked calves.

"Such a glorious little bundle," he murmured. "I never know which part of you to enjoy first."

"This isn't fair," she whispered, resting her hands on his bare shoulders as he cupped one breast between both hands and lowered his head, stroking the hard nipple with a hot, tantalizing tongue.

"All's fair in love," he crooned, his warm breath tormenting her satiny skin. "I adore your breasts; they're so proud and upstanding."

Another shiver ran through her as he transferred his attention to the other breast, moistening the soft curve, cradling it tenderly with firm hands. Emma began to feel that she was hovering on the edge of another world. Her body burned, her secret places were moist, and she could no longer breathe properly. She could feel the heat of Mark's skin beneath her fingers and knew that he, too, was hovering.

As if in response to her thought, Mark raised his head, turned her sideways.

"This is where my problem lies," he murmured, the teasing note in his voice relaxing the charged atmosphere. He was not yet ready to allow passion to engulf them. His fingertips snaked down her back to her buttocks. "While I *am* devoted to your breasts, this pretty little behind is just as beautiful. I can't keep my hands off it."

"I *had* noticed," Emma muttered, trying for the same tone. "You're always patting and squeezing!"

He laughed quietly and proceeded to do both.

"It gets very embarrassing at times," Emma continued, fighting herself for a relative degree of composure. "You did it the other day, when I walked past you in the corridor. You were talking to someone and didn't even pause to say hello, just lunged at me."

"Did I really?" He chuckled. "How shameless! It was a reflex action, I guess."

She couldn't help her own answering chortle as he continued, "There are times when I see you walking through the hospital corridors with that long-legged stride, your arms full of papers, your hair all neat, and your face smothered in those enormous glasses, looking so brisk and purposeful and dignified that I have to reassure myself that under that severe exterior lies my magical bundle."

"And does it?" she murmured, turning around purposefully, insistent hands on his elbows as she decided that the moment was ripe for her playtime.

"Always," he groaned, obeying the demands of her hands as he rose to his feet.

"That's good," Emma stated with quiet satisfaction as her fingers moved deftly over his buttocks and slipped between his thighs, repeating his earlier caresses.

"Don't do this to me," he moaned on a note of delight.

"What's good for the goose . . ." She grinned happily, her fingers busy with the button and zipper of his pants.

"I thought I was supposed to be in charge tonight," Mark muttered plaintively as all his remaining clothes slipped to his ankles under her deft fingers.

"Sit!" she said imperiously, pushing him back into the chair and dropping to her knees.

Mark sighed and began to unpin her hair as she pulled off his shoes and socks.

"Now," she whispered, sliding her hands up his legs with

great deliberation. "Now it's my turn."

Mark's head went back against the seat on a soft groan as her hands and lips worked their own magic, bringing him to the outermost edges of his control until, suddenly, he reached down, caught her under the arms, and pulled her upright.

"Not yet," he whispered, lifting her easily into his arms. "You go on doing that and I'll be no good for anything." Taking the few necessary steps to the bed, he let her go; she bounced on the firm mattress, then lay still, laughing up at him, her hair fanning out on the bedspread.

"I haven't quite finished my naming of parts." The hot coals were there again, turning the mercury of her being into liquid silver as he knelt beside her. "We'll start again here, I think." His tongue lapped her navel, and Emma arched and shifted beneath his touch, no longer capable of coherent thought.

"Tell me what you want, my love," he whispered as his tongue moved lower.

"You," she whimpered, trembling with desire.

"What else?" He had found her now and she could articulate nothing, could only use her body to express herself as he held her on the brink of the precipice.

"Tell me, my own." The words came with urgent insistence, and with a final, deep sigh of willing submission, she gave him what he wanted.

"Take me."

"Into infinite joy, my sweet Emma."

8

"EMMA, YOU WILL *never* do this to me again! Next time, I'll take a cab." Mark looked at his watch for the third time in as many seconds as he stood in the hall, briefcase and suitcase at his feet. Two weeks had passed since the meeting of the Psychiatrists' Association.

"I'm coming," Emma yelled, hurtling down the stairs. "I just can't find my car keys!" She skidded across the polished wood of the hall floor and fell against him. Mark caught her, but he was too irritated either to laugh or to hold her, and merely stood her upright impatiently.

"You can use mine. I'm not going to need them in London."

"Okay! But . . . my glasses! I can't drive without them," she said desperately. Mark, in this mood, made her feel like a chicken without a head.

"They're in the study, for godsake!" he exploded, picking up his luggage as she ran across the hall. "I'm going to the car."

"I'll be with you in a minute," she called, grabbing her glasses from the desk and depositing them on the end of her nose. Money! She had to have cash, credit cards, checkbook! She couldn't drive to the airport and back, penniless.

"Meg, have you seen my purse?" Emma burst through the swinging door into the kitchen as a loud blast of the car horn shivered against the walls.

"On the dresser," Meg said calmly. "What's up with Mark?"

"He thinks he's going to be late for his flight," Emma explained, seizing her purse. "But he's got plenty of time still." The horn blasted again. "I'll see you in a couple of hours," she yelled as she hurled herself out of the house and down the path to collapse breathlessly in the passenger seat of the BMW. Mark had the car in gear before she'd shut the door, and they were squealing down the street as she struggled with her seat belt.

"Never again!" he reiterated fervently. "In the future, I'll find my own way to the airport."

"You're being ridiculous," she said crossly. "You've got acres of time before your flight."

"An acre is a measurement of space, not time," he responded, just as crossly.

"Pedant," she accused.

For a second, there was silence, and then Mark's soft chuckle filled the confined space. "Good Lord, here we are, facing our first separation in the whole three and half months of our married life, and we're snapping at each other's heels like a pair of irritable curs." He placed a hand on her thigh, but she jerked her leg away, not quite willing to make up just yet. He ignored the movement, squeezing the firm flesh with determined pressure.

"I'll be all bruised in the morning," she muttered, trying to sound cross.

"Nonsense!" he scoffed, and with a deep sigh, Emma relaxed beside him.

"You really are neurotic about this time business," she said after a minute.

"We all have our neuroses," he replied blandly.

"I'll miss you, neuroses and all," she murmured, resisting

the urge to snuggle up against him. The traffic required all his attention.

"It was your choice to stay home," he responded evenly.

"I can't be away from the unit for ten days—not so soon after the last time," she said wearily. This was a discussion-bordering-on-argument that they had had too frequently in the last four weeks, and she didn't want to have it again, not now, when he was about to disappear across the Atlantic and she was going to go home to an empty bed.

"As I said, we all have our neuroses." Mark checked his rearview and side mirrors, then pulled out to pass a long, slow truck. "Sam is having a splendid time with Joe," he resumed. "We could have had a few days together, away from domesticity and punctuated by only a minimum of very pleasant work."

"I'm coming on Friday," she said, trying to keep her voice as even as his.

"Yes. In time to hear me present my paper, deliver yours on Saturday, and fly home with me on Monday. You won't even have enough time to recover from the jet lag."

"I need to be sure the unit is in tip-top order for the new boss," she murmured teasingly, deciding not to follow him over the old, well-trodden ground. "After all, Dr. Forrest will take over in two weeks."

"I do not consider myself a violent man," Mark stated carefully as he pulled into the exit lane for the airport, "but somehow, Emma mine, there are times when you bring out my baser instincts!"

"Neurotic chauvinist," she declared. By unspoken agreement, they allowed the argument to be buried, still unresolved, under their laughter, but its resolution required far more time than they had now.

It was eight o'clock on a gray, overcast English morning when Emma emerged from the chaos of Heathrow Airport the following Friday. It was actually three o'clock in the morning, her time, and the two hours of cramped catnapping on the plane could not compensate for the loss of a night's sleep. But in a couple of hours, she would see Mark. She hadn't known it was possible to miss another's presence so much. That vast bed, with all that cold space stretching away from her tightly curled body; eating dinner with Ted and Meg—something she'd done happily for several years but that now seemed strange; even at the hospital, in her unit, everything seemed empty and desolate without Mark's strong arms, his suggestive chuckle, the warm light in his brown eyes that glowed in a special way just for her. She wanted to be with him again, to lock herself into the charmed circle of their wondrous marriage with its flashes of irritation and silly squabbles, its firm strength, its utterly joyful sharing.

The receptionist at the Grosvenor House smiled warmly at Emma, said Dr. Forrest had told them to expect her, apologized for the fact that the room was probably not made up yet, handed her a key and a letter. Emma opened the envelope as she rode upstairs in the elevator with the bellman and felt the color rush into her cheeks. It was not the sort of letter you opened in public! But it *was* the sort of letter you kept forever—a love poem of the earthiest, most uninhibited kind.

The bedroom was full of Mark—the imprint of his body on the rumpled sheets, the clothes neatly hung in the closet, the bathroom redolent with the tang of his shaving cream and cologne, the wet toothbrush, the damp towels hung neatly on the door. But there was one dry towel left on the rack. Emma smiled to herself as she ran water into the tub. Typical of her husband to think of her needs as automatically as he thought of his own.

A bath, clean clothes, and several cups of coffee later, she was as near to her usual self as possible, and went off in search of Mark and the other conference participants. She found them several floors below. Without too much difficulty, she located the conference room where Mark was to give his paper and pushed her way through the chattering group crowding the door.

His back was toward her as he perched negligently on the edge of a long table. As usual, his jacket was draped neatly over the back of a chair, and she watched with covert delight as the long muscles rippled under the custom-made pale blue shirt when he gestured expressively to the surrounding group. Long legs in knife-creased navy slacks stretched out in front of him; liquid joy filled her at the thought that he belonged to her, and she ached for him.

When he turned suddenly, it was as if in response to her thought. A slow smile touched the full lips as he rose quickly, made a vague gesture of excuse to his colleagues, and crossed the room toward her. If this were a movie, Emma thought, this scene would be run in slow motion. She could see the long strides as if on a screen as he loped to her side. Then he was there, taking her hands, drawing her out of the room into the corridor, pressing her against the wall with the length of his body as his hands lifted her face.

"Oh, my darling," he breathed, "I didn't know I could miss anyone so much."

It was such an absolute echo of her own thoughts that her breath caught in her throat. Her face, which he held between his hands, expressed the depth of her response, and with a low groan, he bent his head, captured her mouth, and time and space and the thronged corridor around them ceased to exist.

"Did you get my letter?" he whispered against her lips.

"Mmm," she mumbled. "I made the mistake of opening it in the elevator!" His laughter mingled with hers, and for an instant she pressed against him, trying to meld her body with his.

"Silly girl," he said with a chuckle, tracing the planes of her face with loving, remembering fingers. "You should have known better."

"I know—but I was too tired and disoriented to think clearly, I guess," she said, laughing back.

Mark straightened. "Are you all right, sweet love?"

"Fine." She smiled.

He examined her carefully, touched the slight smudges beneath her eyes. "We have to have lunch with some people after I deliver my paper. Can you hold out? It won't be long."

"Sure I can. The adrenaline's pumping. I can last all day and all evening," she asserted cheerfully.

"After lunch, I'm going to tuck you in for a nap," he stated unequivocally, and she laughed delightedly at his choice of words.

"I'm not Sam, you know."

"Nevertheless, wife, you will take a nap."

"You're getting bossy again, husband."

"So I am." He grinned. "Muscles that have lain dormant for a week need exercising."

"And how," she concurred on a soft murmur.

His eyes became hot coals again, and for a second they stood utterly motionless, transfixed by the intensity of their shared thought. Then Mark shook his head as if to clear his mind, and ran a distracted hand over his face.

"Dear Lord, being married to you is a hazardous business! I can't concentrate on anything else when I'm with you, and I have to present that damn paper. Come on, now, I'm going to introduce you to Michael Beddington. He's saving a seat for you. The sooner this is over, the sooner I can think about other things."

Emma tried to wipe the grin off her face as she responded politely to the courteous greeting of Professor Beddington, an old friend of Mark's and one of the top child psychiatrists in the Western world.

Mark talked to a quiet, attentive audience. Although she had read the paper and worked on it with him, Emma found herself absorbed in the subject, momentarily forgetting that the charismatic, articulate, authoritative man at the head of the table was her husband.

There was a thoughtful silence as he finished, and Emma, looking up from the notes she had been taking, said formally, "Dr. Forrest, may I ask a question?"

"Please do, Dr. Grantham," he answered, a gleam in his eye.

"I was wondering, when you discussed the etiology of autism, why you touched so briefly on the conflict between those who believe that maternal influence is crucial and those who attribute autism to genetics?"

She saw a surprised flash in Mark's eyes and heard a rumble of agreement in the room. Beddington said approvingly, "Good question, Emma."

"Yes, a good question, but a rather uncomfortable one," Mark said dryly. "I agree that that conflict is central to any discussion of autism. However, the emotions it arouses tend to obscure the more pragmatic issues I had hoped to deal with." He looked questioningly around the room. "Do I get the impression that you all would like me to expand on that question?"

"Where do you stand, Dr. Forrest?" an intense young woman piped up.

Mark shot Emma a look that promised retribution, and leaned back in his chair, thumbs hooked casually over his leather belt as he began to talk.

The lively discussion that ensued went on well into the lunch hour scheduled to follow Mark's paper. Eventually, he wrapped up the debate with his usual brisk decisiveness and, as the chattering crowd left the room, came around the table toward her, laughter dancing in his eyes.

"Clearly the loss of a night's sleep hasn't dulled your wits, Emma mine. Why the hell didn't you tell me before that you were going to spring that on me?"

"I didn't know I was until I did," she replied inelegantly. "I'm sorry."

He shrugged. "No matter. I didn't really expect to get away with it. We're having lunch in the Black Sheep around the corner, and we're already late. You know how I hate being late!" His eyes twinkled at her, and she chuckled softly.

"We'd better go, then, hadn't we?"

The stuffy gloom and smoke-hazed atmosphere of the crowded pub did little to alleviate Emma's drowsiness in spite of the animated conversation of their companions. It was the sort of shop talk that she would normally have entered into with enthusiasm—but not this afternoon. She sat in the circle of Mark's arm on a padded leather bench under a diamond-paned window that let in only the minimum of light, and concentrated on keeping her eyes open.

"I think your wife is about to fall asleep, Mark," Michael Beddington said with amusement, and Emma jerked her head off Mark's shoulder, where it had somehow fallen.

"No, I'm not," she denied unconvincingly.

Mark laughed and pulled her to her feet.

"Of course you're not," he teased, "but I think we'll put you somewhere where you can get forty winks, should the need arise."

In the now-tidy room, Mark disappeared into the bathroom, and Emma, with a groan of contentment, collapsed on the bed.

"Hey!" He came back into the room. "Bath first."

"Already had one," she muttered, curling into a tight, resistant ball as he began to undress her.

He laughed quietly and continued with deft efficiency to take off her clothes before lifting and depositing her in the tub of hot, scented water. Emma watched through half-closed eyes as he rolled up the sleeves of his shirt and dropped to his knees beside the tub. She made no further protest, but gave herself up to the gentle, caressing hands moving over her body, which was incapable of any response but an occasional soft purr of contentment. He dried her, carried her to the bed, pulled back the covers, and rolled her onto her stomach. The next instant, she felt his hands on her neck, his firm fingers feeling for the tight, bunched muscles and massaging them. Then his hands moved over her shoulders, her arms, down her back. She felt the gentle stroking on her buttocks, sliding between her thighs, back again, but desire only flickered like a dying candle, and with another quiet laugh, he patted her gently and pulled the covers over her.

"Sweet dreams, sweet love." His lips brushed the nape of her neck, and she slipped into unconsciousness.

Emma awoke in a dark and empty room and lay still, getting her bearings before rolling over to flick on the bedside lamp. A large sheet of paper lay on the pillow beside her, the message in Mark's bold, black script laughing up at her: "Back by six o'clock. Don't move one inch from that bed, Emma mine!"

She grinned, stretched, yawned, and pushed back the covers, heading for the bathroom where she brushed her teeth, washed her face, and brushed her long, straight hair until it shone. She was finishing her unpacking when the sound of the key in the door heralded Mark's return.

"Good grief," he murmured, regarding her robed figure through hooded eyes. "Seems that you've forgotten how to read."

Wordlessly, Emma slipped off her robe and followed the direction of his imperative forefinger, which pointed toward the bed.

"That's better," he said approvingly, turning to the closet with his jacket. "We have some unfinished business to attend to."

Much, much later Emma arched her body in a luxurious stretch, propped herself up on one elbow and leaned over him, her hair enclosing them both in a silky, fragrant tent. "What now, my darling?" she murmured, stroking his drooping eyelids with the tip of her tongue in a feathery movement.

"Don't do that," he groaned, running a lazy hand over her back. "I'm all played out for a while."

"But what now?" she repeated, continuing to explore his face with the caresses of her tongue.

He lifted her away from him, struggled upright, and leaned back against the headboard. "We can stay here and call room service, go downstairs for dinner, or go out on London town." He tapped the choices off on his fingers.

"We don't have to have dinner with anyone?"

"Not tonight, but it's our only free evening, I'm afraid. Tomorrow and Sunday are going to be all work."

"Oh." She tried not to sound disappointed.

"Can't be helped, sweet," he said briskly. "I've had two free evenings this week, but you weren't around for them."

Emma bit her lip. "You're still annoyed about that, aren't you?"

Mark sighed heavily. "I suppose I must be; otherwise I wouldn't keep bringing it up."

"I wish you'd try to understand—" she began, but he interrupted her brusquely.

"I have tried, Emma, and I still can't find one convincing reason why you couldn't bring yourself to leave the unit for a week!"

"There's a lot going on at the moment," she said quietly.

"We're trying to implement the new budget requirements, and there are a lot of new staff members who don't know what's what. I can't afford inadvertent errors. We're not in compliance with most of the hospital's rules and regulations as it is, but at least that's deliberate and I can take responsibility."

"What do you mean you're not in compliance?" Mark frowned.

"I shouldn't have said that, should I? Not to the new medical director," she said flatly. "I forgot for a moment. Sorry."

Mark's lips tightened; the warmth died out of his brown eyes. "At the moment, you're in bed with me," he said stiffly, "and I still want to know what you mean. I'm aware that you manipulate the system when necessary, but that isn't the same as not being in compliance."

Emma shrugged. He had to know sometime. "I get away with as much as I can openly, but there's a whole lot that the administration knows nothing about. It's the only way I can fulfill the contract, and if I don't fulfill it, the unit will go. You know that!"

"And if it ever comes out that you're not in compliance with the basic rules and regulations, you'll lose your job, and that'll be the end of the unit as it now stands, anyway," he replied fiercely.

"It's Catch Twenty-two. I've lived with it for three years, but now perhaps you can understand why I hate being out of touch."

"You bet I do! I'm amazed you're able to sleep nights!" He flung himself out of bed and stalked into the bathroom; soon the sound of the shower filled the room.

Emma sighed. She'd known this was going to have to come out at some point. She couldn't have left Mark in the dark in the way she had his predecessors. If something disastrous had happened under their administration, only she would have suffered, but if a problem occurred now, her husband's position would be untenable.

"You realize that the JCAH is coming in July?" Mark reappeared, drying himself vigorously.

Emma nodded. The Joint Commission for the Accreditation of Hospitals was the most important organization in the life of any hospital. Without the commission's accreditation, the state would withdraw all funds from St. Anne's, and no self-respecting professional would continue working there. Not that St. Anne's was in any danger of losing its accreditation, but there would be hell to pay if some of the things Emma and her subordinates did—and more important, didn't do—in the kids' unit came out. She was actually well prepared for the inspection, and by July she would have the other members of her team prepared, too. They had survived a JCAH visit once before and had come out smelling like a rose garden, secrets still intact. She saw no reason why they shouldn't do the same this time, but that wasn't going to comfort Mark, who, as chief practical administrator, would have his head on the block.

"How far out of line are you?" He pulled on his shorts with an aggressive tug.

"In some things, far out," she admitted candidly, "but you won't have to worry if you'll just let me handle things as I always have."

"The hell I won't!" He thumped onto the bed, dragging on his socks. "We're going through your *Policies and Pro-*

cedures Manual as soon as we get home and, by God, it had better be in order!"

Emma grimaced; she didn't even know where the blessed manual was. "Is that the big blue one?" she asked with an innocent smile.

Mark gave vent to an incoherent exclamation, dragged the covers off her, seized her under the arms, and hauled her across his knees, face down. "No, it's the red one! As you damn well ought to know!"

"Let me go, Mark!" She struggled against the restraining pressure in the small of her back and heard his sudden soft laugh.

"Let's see you wriggle out of this one, my little eel." His fingernails scribbled a path down her spine, and she quivered, her breath catching as his free hand slipped over her buttocks, slid across her thigh, played in the hollow behind her knee.

"I'm not comfortable," she mumbled desperately through the curtain of hair falling over her face.

"I wonder why not?" Amusement rippled in the mellow voice as his hand slithered between her thighs, stroking the silky, sensitive skin. "I'm doing my best."

"It's not good enough!"

His burst of laughter peeled through the room. "Even *in extremis,* Emma mine, you're not short of an answer!"

He turned her right side up and fell back on the bed, holding her on top of him.

"You've really gotten away with it for three years?" There was awed amazement in his voice.

"Even through the last JCAH inspection," she asserted. "I know what I'm doing, Mr. Medical Director."

"You *have* to." A serious note had crept into his voice. "But we've got to work on this together, Emma. I can't go into anything blind."

"Why do you think I told you?" She lay still against his length.

"I suppose that explains at least some of your reasons for not wanting me to take this job," he said thoughtfully.

"Well, I did offer a few hints," Emma observed levelly. "But does it also explain why I hate leaving the unit? It's not really a neurosis."

"It explains everything," he said flatly. "However"— Mark sat up, putting her firmly on the bed beside him—"in my dual role as your husband and your administrator, Emma Grantham, I have to tell you that something must be done."

"Like what?" she shrugged helplessly. "As I said, it's a perfect Catch Twenty-two."

"I can't make any suggestions until I find out the full horror story—but we'll start with your *Policies and Procedures Manual*. What color is it?"

"Blue . . . no, red." She squealed, scooting across the bed as he reached for her with swift, avenging hands.

"I guess it's going to have to be room service," Emma murmured, lying subdued and exhausted beneath him some time later.

Mark stretched out a languid hand and picked up the menu, examining it with a frown. "I'm not inclined to experiment tonight," he muttered. "We'll settle for a bottle of Côte de Beaune and a couple of steaks, okay?"

"Whatever you say, husband," she murmured docilely,

but her fingers were far from docile as they ran up his backbone while he reached for the phone.

9

MARK COULDN'T POSSIBLY really want this information! Emma nibbled at her thumbnail as she examined the memo from the medical director that for the past month had lain carelessly disregarded under a pile of papers on her desk. It was a request to all unit heads—actually, it was a directive, but Mark's directives always read like requests—for a statistical report on the number of therapy sessions in the last month that had been extended beyond the statutory hour, and the reasons for each extension. She had given the memo a quick glance when it came across her desk four weeks ago, decided it couldn't be that important, and forgotten about it. Now she was beginning to wonder uneasily if that had been wise. The report was due tomorrow morning, and she had just spent an uncomfortable half-hour in the cafeteria listening to her colleagues' jubilant announcements that their reports had hit the internal mail on time. She hadn't even started hers yet, and it would be a mammoth task, since extended sessions on the kids' unit were the rule rather than the exception. They were all documented, of course, but bringing the material together in a single report would take forever—and why did he want it, anyway? There was enough paper drifting around this institution as it was!

Emma reached for the phone and then decided against it. Trying to get through Edie, Mark's formidable secretary, was like bearding a lioness in her den; she'd do better face-to-face.

"Can I talk to you for a minute, Em?"

Emma stopped in her tracks, memo in hand, as Bella poked her head around the door. "Sure, Bella. Problems?"

"Not exactly," the girl answered. She was wearing much less makeup these days, Emma noticed, although her fingernails were still scarlet.

"You want to sit down?" Emma dropped casually into a chair by the window, waving a hand toward the other chair in silent invitation.

"It's about my medications," Bella muttered, sitting on the arm of the chair, half-facing the door; clearly she was not yet ready to settle in, Emma reflected.

"About reducing them?" she queried quietly.

"Yes. I mean . . . well . . . fifty milligrams! Supposing I get . . . I get lost again, Em?" The anxiety in the girl's voice filled the small room as she inspected her long, talonlike nails.

"If I see you getting lost again, Bella, I'll up the dosage so fast you won't even know it's happened." Emma spoke with soft but firm reassurance. "I don't think you will. I can't guarantee it, of course, but I'm willing to give it a try, if you are."

"Yeah," was the muttered response. "Only . . . can I talk to Mark about it?"

"Need a second opinion?" Emma smiled, pushing the phone toward the girl. "Call him—extension two forty-four."

"But he might think . . ." The girl's voice drifted off with uncharacteristic hesitancy.

"Tell you what—I'm going up there now. Why don't I

ask him to come down later?" Emma offered.

"D'you think he will?" Bella stood up, jamming her hands into her pockets.

"Of course he will," Emma declared with conviction. Mark would never turn down such a request, however occupied, or preoccupied, he might be.

"Okay . . . Thanks, Em."

"You're welcome, Bella." She watched as the girl left the office, her face hopeful. These were the moments that made all the agony, the one step forward, two steps back, worthwhile, Emma reflected.

Edie looked at her suspiciously as she walked into the reception area outside Mark's office. "He's very busy, Dr. Grantham, and left instructions that he wasn't to be disturbed," she said firmly.

Emma glanced across at the door leading to the medical director's office. "The red light isn't on," she observed pleasantly.

"Well, he must have forgotten to turn it on," the secretary responded stubbornly. "I'm sorry, but he said specifically, no interruptions."

"Edie, I'm sure Dr. Forrest will see me," Emma replied smoothly, an agreeable smile masking her underlying irritation. Hitching herself onto the desk, she reached across, ignoring Edie's indignant gasp, and punched the intercom button.

"Yes?" The short, sharp response hung in the air, and Emma grinned to herself.

"Dr. Grantham is here to see you, Dr. Forrest. She requests just a few moments of your very valuable time," she said silkily.

"Then she'd better come in, hadn't she?" The low, reso-nant voice carried more than a hint of amusement. Emma smiled sweetly at Edie and marched into Mark's office.

"I tell you, Mark," she said, as she leaned back against the door, closing it with her weight, "one of these days, I'm going to give in to the urge to put my tongue out at that woman!"

Mark laughed. "Edie's protective instincts can get a little out of hand, I admit. But she's very good at her job."

Emma gazed at him as he rocked back in his swivel chair, hands linked negligently behind his head, one leg thrown casually over the other. He was *so* beautiful!

"Come here." A commanding finger beckoned.

"Now what have you got in mind?" she asked warily.

"You haven't said good morning to me yet. In fact, to speak candidly, you were exceedingly bad tempered this morning!" He was giving her that lazy smile again, and she was melting under it, her bones disintegrating beneath the loving sun of his all-encompassing appraisal.

"Well, you have only yourself to blame," she declared with a totally unsuccessful attempt at severity, "if you're such a workaholic that you have to attend breakfast meet-ings at seven-thirty in the morning! I like to wake up slowly, not be hurled into a new day at six A.M."

"I know." A sensuous smile curved his lips. "You're wonderful in the morning—all pink and pearly and cross, and then you get all soft and cuddly and absolutely edible."

This was hopeless, Emma thought as desire engulfed her. How could she possibly talk about work when he did this to her?

"Now, are you coming over here or do I have to come

and get you?" He was laughing openly, fully aware of her reaction.

She moved slowly around the desk and allowed him to pull her down onto his knee. He tipped her backward until her head rested in the crook of his arm and traced a lazy, caressing finger over the planes of her face.

"You know perfectly well that that lioness out there is going to decide it's time to rescue her cub and come marching in here with something that requires your signature immediately," she said impishly.

Mark reached across the desk and pressed the switch that activated the red light above his door. "Not even Edie will come in now." He grinned. "Where were we?"

"I was about to say good morning," she murmured.

"So you were." His lips took hers with the firm, cool possession that, as always, brought prickles of anticipation tingling across the entire surface of her skin. Mark's hand slipped inside the open collar of her blouse, kneading the soft roundness of her breast, tantalizing the hard, expectant nipple.

"Good morning, Emma," he said softly. Pulling her up into a sitting position, he recline back in his chair, holding her waist lightly. "Much as I would like to believe you braved Edie just for that, I'm sure you had some other reason."

"I did." She sighed. "But you're going to have to let me up. This concerns Dr. Forrest and Dr. Grantham."

"I don't like the sound of that." He released her reluctantly, and she marched to the other side of his desk.

"What *is* this, Mark?" She held out the memo.

He took it, read it with a frown, and handed it back.

"Seems quite clear to me."

"You don't seriously expect me to do that report, surely?"

"Well . . . yes, I do," he said, puzzled. "Everyone else has."

"Maybe so, but I extend sessions as a matter of course. Everyone knows that, you more than anyone."

"All the more reason for you to write a report. What's the problem, Emma?"

"The problem is that I don't have the time to push this sort of unnecessary paper around," she declared.

"Aren't you making a rather biased assumption there?" His face had that rigid, taut look again, and her heart sank. Clearly, this was not going to be a comfortable discussion.

"Well, why do you want it?" she asked reasonably.

"Partly for the JCAH and partly because I need to find out how much of it is going on," he responded promptly.

"So you can crack down, I suppose," Emma grumbled, striding to the window.

"That is *not* the reason! Extending a session is against the rules, sure, but if there's a need to change the rule, I have to have some evidence. Would you come away from that window? I don't like talking to your back!"

"Actually, you were *shouting* at my back." She swung around.

"I was not shouting, but there are times when you make me want to," he said tightly. "I need that information from everybody. Why should you be exempt?"

"Because it's too much paperwork! I have enough to do without scurrying around on this sort of nonsense. Felix understood that; even Jenner did. Neither of them would have insisted."

"Well, I do insist," he stated flatly, as their angry eyes met across the room. Then Mark suddenly chuckled. "Darling, Felix indulged you hopelessly, and Jenner was scared stiff of you. I'm not scared of you, and the only place I'm prepared to indulge you is in bed! I need those statistics from the kids' unit more than I need them from anywhere else, but even if I didn't, how would it look if you were the only unit head absolved from this responsibility? You're my wife, sweet, and therefore we have to be absolutely scrupulous."

"I knew this wouldn't work." Emma shook her head in frustration. "Instead of making my job easier, you're actually making it harder. I'm beginning to feel as if I have no autonomy at all."

"Don't be ridiculous," he said shortly. "I know this is a boring, tedious task, but it has to be done. No one else has objected."

"I don't feel like playing Simon Says right now," she retorted. Mark drew in his breath sharply, and it occurred to Emma, rather belatedly, that she had probably gone too far.

"All, right, I'm sorry," she said quickly. "That was unreasonable."

"Damn right it was!"

"It's just that I'm snowed under with work, and this seemed like the last straw." Her voice faded. The combination of new staff members on the unit and the lack of Mark's active presence was rapidly driving her to a point of desperation that she had kept secret from him, knowing that he needed all his energies to get on top of his new job.

Mark's eyes softened, and the stiffness left his body. She waited for him to reach for her, to enfold her with his warm strength as he always did when she finally admitted her difficulties. But this time, he didn't. He stood up and drove his hands very firmly into the side pockets of his dark brown slacks, as if that were the only way he could keep them still, and casually perched on the edge of the enormous desk.

"Are you ready now, Dr. Grantham, to talk sensibly about getting some help on the unit?"

"Who?" She didn't bother to argue the point. There was no alternative; the last six weeks had taught her that.

"Craig," Mark said calmly.

She frowned. "But he's not a consultant here."

"I talked to him a couple of weeks ago, on the assumption that at some point soon you would be forced to face reality! He's willing to offer the kids' unit fifteen hours a week. You and he get along very well, Emma. He's not going to interfere in the way you run the program, but he will take some of the therapy overload off your shoulders."

"Leaving me with more time to push paper." She sighed.

"It goes with the job, sweet love," Mark said evenly. "If you want to do just therapy, you should move into private practice."

"Perhaps I should." Emma chewed her bottom lip miserably. "At least it would relieve the tension for *us*."

"You've got to be kidding!" Mark exclaimed. "Don't you realize how impossible you'd be to live with if you gave up the unit?"

"Even more impossible than I am already?" A slight smile touched her lips as she accepted the truth of his words.

"Come here." He took his hands out of his pockets and opened his arms.

"I was beginning to think you'd never ask," she murmured against his chest as, at long last, he held her.

"I wasn't aware I'd asked." He chuckled softly, clasping her head tightly. "I just wish I knew how to handle you. There are times when I think I'll have to wait forever before you'll admit that you have more work than you can handle, and yet I know that if I push you, you'll retreat even farther into your corner. What do you *want* me to do, sweet?"

"Just carry on as you are," she whispered. "I can't change my personality or my ways of working, any more than you can change yours. But I know you're there for me. I may not always appear to take advantage of it, but I *do* know it."

"That's enough for me." He took her face between his hands, kissed her gently. "We'll work this one out, Emma mine."

"Yes." She nodded her agreement. "This one and all the others, my love."

"And there are going to be many others, I'm afraid," Mark said softly.

"They call it marriage, I think." Smiling, Emma moved out of the loving circle of his arms. "I can't get this report done by tomorrow." She picked up the memo from the desk where she had dropped it earlier. "Unless, of course, I work all night." Her tone was brisk, businesslike, and Mark instantly responded to her new tack. They still had to resolve this professional issue.

"I can give you until Monday morning. We'll do it together over the weekend."

"In that case, I'll need authorization to remove the charts

from the hospital."

"Put it in writing."

"Pompous bureaucrat!" Emma grinned, reaching for the memo pad on Mark's desk. She scribbled furiously for a moment, then tore off the sheet and handed it to him.

Mark read it, scrawled his initials, and gave it back. "On your way out, ask Edie to make a copy of this for my files."

"I think I've just been dismissed from the holy presence," Emma teased. He lunged for her, and she dodged behind the desk. "You touch me, Mr. Medical Director, and I'll scream!" Laughing helplessly, she sidled around the room as he stalked her. "Think what fun Edie will have with that!"

"Get out of here, Emma Grantham!" Mark was laughing too much himself to exact the penalty he had in mind, and she reached the door safely. "Just one more thing," he said suddenly as she grasped the doorknob. "Do you think you could find your *Policies and Procedures Manual*? It's the red one—remember?"

"How did you know I'd lost it?" Mark had been asking for quite some time when they could go through the manual together, and she thought her discreet evasions had been successful.

"My sweet Emma," he said, suddenly serious, "you may be able to pull the wool over the eyes of most of the world, but not over mine! Find it! Okay?"

"It *has* to be somewhere." She shrugged. "And don't tell me I'm not in compliance, because it's not prominently displayed in the nurses' station. I know that."

"Then I won't tell you," he responded evenly. "Just find it!"

"Yes, sir! Right away, sir!" Her hand touched her forehead in mock salute, and she slipped from the room. The next instant her head popped around the door again. "Is it safe to come back in for a minute?" she asked in an exaggerated whisper in deference to Edie sitting rigidly at her desk. Mark's eyes danced as he looked at her. She was the most outrageously irreverent creature!

"For godsake, come in and shut the door," he whispered back urgently. "Abominable woman! What is it now?"

"I am *not* abominable," Emma declared. "Bella wants to talk to you about her medications. I want to reduce them to a maintenance dose, but she wants a second opinion."

"She *doesn't* want to decide the material of my tie?" Mark murmured, fingering the garment deliberately.

"Not this time." Emma was quite serious now. "She's hovering on the verge of agreeing, but she needs you to tip the balance."

"I'll drop by this afternoon," he responded, "before they go to dinner."

"I won't be there; it's my turn for the early night with Sam. Do what you can. She's ready."

"Will do, Emma mine."

She nodded, satisfied, and left the room.

"Where is everyone?" Mark's cheery shout from the hall that evening brought Emma's head up from the stack of papers on the desk in the study.

"In here," she called back. The door opened, and Mark stood smiling, his jacket hooked on one finger and flung negligently over his shoulder in deference to the warm, late May evening.

"Hi," she said, watching as he took in the scene. He glanced at Sam, who stood rigidly in the corner of the room, and raised his eyebrows interrogatively. She shrugged, shook her head wryly.

"How long?" he mouthed.

Emma held up four fingers, glanced at her watch as she had done unhappily every thirty seconds for the last three minutes and then held up one finger, mouthing back, "One to go."

Mark nodded, tossed his jacket onto the couch, and perched on the desk. Four minutes was a stiff sentence by their standards. Sam had clearly upset his mother! "Any mail?" he asked conversationally.

"Only bills," she replied easily, handing him the pile. "I thought you'd paid the dentist."

"I thought you had," he responded, flicking through the envelopes.

"Well, judging by the plaintive note, neither of us did."

"I'll do it, then. I've got a heap of checks to write, anyway."

"Fine." Emma looked at her watch. "You're all through, Sam," she said quietly.

The little boy turned around, his eyes—almost but not quite Emma's shade of violet—overlarge and glistening, his lower lip tremulous.

"Hello, Sam." Mark smiled, as if the child had just walked into the room.

"'Lo," Sam muttered.

"How about a kiss?" Mark patted his knee invitingly. Sam jumped instantly into his arms as Emma watched. Why was it that the sight of them together weakened her knees, melted her insides? She could share Sam with Mark absolutely, although the child was not his.

"Care to tell me about it?" Mark asked, tilting the boy's small square chin.

Sam mumbled something of which only the words "porch roof" were clear. But it was quite enough for Mark, who shook his head in exasperation, "Sam Richards, how many times do we have to go through this? Going out on that roof is very dangerous!"

"Forgot." Sam offered his usual excuse.

"I think it's time we did something to help you remember." Mark set him briskly on his feet. "Go into the kitchen and find the tape and the thumbtacks."

"What color thumbtacks?" Sam asked with a puzzled frown. "We got red 'n' green ones."

"You choose."

"Why does he keep climbing out there?" Emma exclaimed in frustration. "He knows it scares the living daylights out of me, and he also knows it's dangerous—we've explained that often enough!"

"I rather suspect that that's where the irresistible attraction lies," Mark observed dryly.

Sam reappeared, mission accomplished, and Mark held out his hand. "Let's go upstairs now."

The child took Mark's hand, and they left the room, followed by a very curious Emma. A low window in Sam's bedroom stood open onto the flat roof outside, and Mark closed it firmly.

"Now, Sam, we're going to put two pieces of tape across the window, one at the top and one at the bottom, and we'll fasten them with the thumbtacks. Do you want to do it?"

Sam nodded and entered with enthusiasm into what he clearly saw as a game. Only when they had finished the task did he ask with a frown, "Why?"

"Next time you decide you want to go out there, you'll have to take the tape off," Mark explained carefully. "And you'll remember why it's there, won't you?"

"Mmmm," the child murmured. Then he added thoughtfully, "Could do it, though."

"Sure you could," Mark agreed, "but if you do, you'll remember that while you *can* do it, you *may* not."

There was a short silence, and then Mark dropped onto his heels and took Sam's chubby hands in his. "If you do decide to go out there again, Sam, you will earn a stiffer punishment than four minutes in the corner. Do you understand?"

Sam chewed his lip in a way that reminded Mark so forcibly of Emma that he had to struggle to keep his face grave.

"Awright," the small voice muttered, and the little figure, with a sudden movement, turned and lunged into his closet, emerging with a large plastic bucket that he upended in a noisy shower of Lego in the middle of the room. "Gonna make a airplane," he stated. "You gonna help me, Mark?"

"Right now, Sam, I'm going to make myself a large scotch and soda and read the paper." Mark smiled. "You build the airplane and bring it down when you've finished."

"That was clever," Emma said admiringly as they walked down the stairs. "I wonder if it'll work."

"If it doesn't," Mark said evenly, "we're going to have to use sterner measures, I'm afraid."

Emma made a rueful face. "It would be so much easier just to put a lock on the window."

"It would," he agreed, going over to the bar in the living room, "but the only lesson Sam would learn from that is that if we want to stop him forcibly from doing something he wants to do, we can. That's not really what we're trying to teach him."

Emma laughed. "No, self-discipline, a sense of responsibility, decision-making skills—right?"

"Right." He laughed back, handing her a glass. "And on a similar theme, did you find that manual this afternoon?"

"I didn't have time to look for it," she confessed. "I'll find it tomorrow, promise."

Mark sighed. "I'm really trying not to be difficult about this, Emma, but I have to know what you're doing in the kids' unit. I can also help you, if you'll let me. I want to go through the written policies and procedures and see how they correlate with your actual practices. I'm willing to bend the rules, but I have to know where and when it's being done."

"And authorize it," she said slowly.

"Yes," he replied firmly. "Don't you realize that if you're legitimate, so to speak, a lot of the strain will be lifted? For starters, you won't panic about leaving the place for a few days."

"I hadn't really thought of that." Emma dropped onto the sofa and took a long sip of her drink. "To tell you the truth, I rather assumed that you would just create bureaucratic hell when you saw how far out of line we are."

"You're making a lot of assumptions these days, Emma mine. Sometimes I get the feeling that you see me as an enemy."

"Oh, of course I don't, love. It's just that you're part of the administration now. I can't help making a distinction between my husband and my medical director. You've only been on the job for a few weeks; it's bound to get easier." She was uncomfortably aware that she sounded much more convinced of that than she felt.

"It's not going to get any easier if you don't start trusting me," he said grimly.

Emma sprang to her feet, heedless of her drink spilling over the rim of the glass. "What do you mean? I trust you implicitly!"

"You trust me as your husband, but not as a colleague any longer." The blunt statement seemed to take on a tangible quality as it hung between them.

Then Emma spoke quietly, almost as if the words were being dragged out of her. "But most of the time you're not my colleague any longer. You're my boss."

"Dammit, Emma!" he exploded with an anger fueled by a deep hurt. "Why should that matter? It's a technicality, that's all."

"You once said it was more than that," she reminded him calmly.

"Well, it is and it isn't," he said in exasperation. "But if that's the way you see the situation, then maybe I'll start living up to your expectations."

"What do you mean?" she asked, suddenly wary, sensing that he was as angry as she had ever seen him.

"I mean that if that manual is not on my desk by five o'clock tomorrow afternoon, you will find out just how much of a bureaucratic hell I can create," he stated with tight-lipped authority.

"I have some letters to write." Emma stalked out of the room and sat down miserably at the desk in the study. Such arguments were becoming run-of-the-mill these days, and she couldn't decide whose fault they really were. On the one hand, she was very uncomfortable with their adversarial positions in the hospital and did see him as her chief administrator—but those were facts, facts that Mark frequently seemed to deny. Half the time he behaved as if nothing had changed, and the rest of the time he played the bureaucrat as he had to. As a result, they were both confused, and their confusion found an outlet in these ridiculous, hurtful, pointless squabbles.

The space between her body and Mark's in the wide bed seemed infinite that night as Emma lay stiff, cold, and still, gazing wide-eyed into the darkness. She knew he was doing the same; one of them had to break the deadlock. She slid her hand across the intervening gap, touched his back with tentative fingertips. Mark didn't move toward her, but he hadn't moved away from her, either. She increased the pressure, feeling for the hard line of his spine.

"You would really think that a couple of psychiatrists could sort things out a bit better than this." His voice cut the darkness, neutral, conversational almost.

"We're only human, love," she responded in much the same tone, although her body surged with relief.

"There are times when the human condition becomes singularly unpleasant," Mark declared.

"There are also times when it is utterly blissful," she murmured, as her body followed her fingers and she molded herself against his back, relaxing with a sigh into his body warmth.

"Emma, you are the most infuriating, exasperating, awe-inspiring, spell-weaving enchantress!" Mark rolled over, pulling her beneath him, his hands parting her thighs with a no-nonsense efficiency.

"It's fortunate I married an infuriating, exasperating, awe-inspiring wizard, then," she said smugly, adjusting herself easily as he raised her hips.

"You figure we deserve each other, do you?" he muttered into her ear as his tongue sent her into paroxysms of wild sensation, alternately stroking and plundering the tender sensitivity until she was thrashing beneath him, her legs curled around his waist, pressing him into the cleft of her body.

"Mark?" she whispered, in a sudden, urgent plea.

"What is it, my own love?" He raised his head, smiled from the other world they were both inhabiting.

She shook her head incoherently.

"Say it. Tell me what you want, my sweet," he demanded in a whisper as urgent as her own.

"You," she breathed.

"What else?"

Their eyes locked, and he moved with infinite slowness within her, tantalizing her, holding them both on the furthest edge of delight until she whispered, "Take me."

He groaned, seizing her mouth in a fierce, deeply demanding kiss that expressed utter commitment. The starburst of their shared climax shuddered through their fused bodies.

10

EMMA WAS NEVER sure exactly what it was that brought the hairs on the back of her neck to prickly life as she sat at her desk in the small office opening off the dayroom at lunchtime the next day. It could have been the silence—a few minutes earlier the laughing voices of the children as they came in for lunch had rung through the unit, heads had popped in greeting around her door, which, as always, was ajar—but it wasn't just that. There was a quality to this silence that drew her from her chair to walk softly toward the dayroom. The sight that met her eyes momentarily froze her as an almost hallucinatory panic rooted her feet to the floor.

A group of children had formed a circle around two fifteen-year-old boys, each of whom held a knife, the wicked stiletto blades caught in a shaft of sunlight from the far window. They were both crouched, knees bent in a relaxed state of readiness.

She was the only adult in the dayroom. Strange, disconnected voices reached her from the "quiet room" down the hall where several children were talking with one of the attendants; one or two other children were resting on their beds in the dormitories down the corridor; Delia was in the nurses' station, but that damn television monitor had *still* not been fixed! No one could see what was going on out here, and there was no time to call for assistance if the catastrophe was to be averted. Emma's thought processes were *very* fast—too fast to be analyzed at this moment. The only important fact seemed to be that José and Mario were waiting to spring, still assessing each other.

She broke through the circle. "Hold it, both of you!" Her arm went up between them, and in that instant, sharp pain lacerated her skin.

Both knives fell to the floor with a dull clash, and two stricken youths turned to her.

"Em . . . you all right, Em?" The confused stammers reached her through a haze of pain and shock.

"Somebody get out here," she shouted, and immediately the room filled with wide-eyed, alarmed members of the unit staff.

"Phil," she turned to one of the young attendants, "get these two into a seclusion room together. Make sure they've got nothing on them. And if either of you does anything but talk," she turned with deliberate, calculated fierceness on the two confused, shocked youngsters, "I'll make damn sure you regret it!"

Blood from her cut arm dripped sticky and inexorably onto the floor as Phil led the two boys away.

"We need to look at that, Em." Delia put her hand under Emma's arm. Emma shook it off.

"Get me a towel or something," she said with swift impatience. "I have other things to deal with right now." Delia went into the nurses' station and reached for a towel. "Somebody call Mark," she said briskly. "Emma needs stitches."

Emma wanted to sit down, but decided that if she did she'd never get up again, so she remained on her feet, wrapped the towel around her arm to stem the strange flow of blood that seemed to have nothing to do with her, and faced the group.

"I want some answers," she began, "Why did that happen? And how did José and Mario get those knives in here?"

There was a short silence, and then the story began to unfold as the shocked, stunned group came to life in a babble of explanatory voices. A family feud had been brewing for weeks. The fight had begun on the street during their last weekend pass and had been stopped by a policeman; but José and Mario had only been waiting for a chance to continue it.

Mark walked swiftly into the unit in response to the urgent summons while Emma was still trying to piece the story together. He took a second to absorb the scene, saw Emma, gray-faced, swaying slightly on the outskirts of the circle of sitting children, listened for a moment, and then made his move.

"Emma needs to have her arm taken care of," he said briskly. "Phil and Joyce, you want to take over here? Get this group calmed down."

"I'm not through yet," Emma protested fiercely as he took her arm.

"You're all through," he responded calmly, and whisked her into the nurses' station.

"Who's on medical duty?" Mark asked Delia as he unwrapped the soggy towel with gentle fingers.

"Jim Lester. He's being paged," Delia responded. "I'm making tea, on the assumption that the old-fashioned remedies are often the best."

"Put plenty of sugar in it." He examined the cut carefully. "You need about six stitches, sweet."

"Just bandage it," Emma said wearily. "And I don't like

sugar in my tea."

"You're going to have six stitches in your arm and three spoonfuls of sugar in your tea," Mark declared coolly. "And then you can tell me all about this debacle."

"I think I'm going to be sick." Cold sweat beaded her forehead as a wave of dizzy nausea suddenly washed through her.

Mark pushed her down onto one of the high stools at the counter, grabbed a stainless steel bowl, and held her head as she retched miserably until the attack had passed. He took the damp cloth Delia handed him and gently wiped Emma's face.

"All right now?"

"Sort of," she managed weakly. "Sorry about that."

"You've had a nasty shock, sweet," he said quietly. "Drink some of this." He held the cup to her lips, and she sipped obediently. The hot, sweet liquid had an instant restorative effect.

"Get the pharmacy to send up some Valium—I.M.— Delia, will you?" he said over his shoulder, still holding the cup.

"If that Valium's for me, I don't want it," Emma protested. The last thing she needed was an intramuscular injection of Valium. "I'll be perfectly all right once I've finished this tea."

"Should I be at all interested in what you want—as opposed to what you need—I'll ask you, my love," he said crisply. Delia tried to hide a smile and reached for the phone.

"Somebody need my services?" The bright voice of Jim Lester served only to add to Emma's misery. The one thing she had dreaded in the last three years had finally happened. If only Delia hadn't called Mark, if only they had let her just bandage the arm and get whatever treatment she needed outside the hospital, if only they had let her deal with this mess in the privacy of the closed community of the unit! But then, life was paved with if onlys. The lid had really blown now, and only she knew exactly what that was going to mean, both for herself, and for Mark.

"We can probably do it with six, don't you reckon, Mark?"

Jim looked up from his close examination of her arm.

"Mmm," he concurred, hitching another stool out from under the counter. "Now, Emma mine, hold my hand, forget what Jim's doing to your injured arm, and, if you feel up to it, start talking."

"I hate needles," she muttered as she watched Jim prepare to stitch the cut. She felt the strong, reassuring squeeze as Mark pressed her hand.

"Tell me what happened. It'll take your mind off what's going on." The voice was gently insistent and, with resignation in her soul, she told the story.

Mark heard her out in frowning silence, asking when she had finished, "Why was there no one observing in the dayroom?"

"We don't keep them under constant surveillance, Mark. This is an open unit; the kids come and go as they please. Don't tell me you've forgotten that?"

"And the monitor?" He glanced up at the dead television screen, high on the wall.

"It's broken," she explained dully. "I've sent down endless requisition orders to maintenance, but you know how slow they are to respond."

"I also know that when you want something done, you get it," he observed dryly. "However, we'll leave that one for the moment. Why on earth didn't you call for help, instead of taking them on single-handed?"

"There wasn't time," Emma said flatly. "I had a split second and I took it. If I'd hesitated, there would have been a bloodbath."

A slight smile touched his lips. "I don't know whether you're very, very brave or very, very foolhardy, my sweet." He sighed and shook his head. "The one thing I do know is that our security guards are going to get hell over this one. How the devil did they let those knives get past the check?"

Emma gulped, took a deep breath, and plunged. "The guards didn't have the opportunity to find them. We've been doing our own security checks for the last two years."

"What?" The color drained from Mark's face, and his fingers tightened painfully on her hand.

"The system the security guards use is undignified at best, humiliating at worst," she said quietly. "We operate an honor system backed up with random checks. It's the same principle you and I use with Sam and the porch roof, if you remember."

He said nothing; in fact, he seemed incapable of speech. "Look, love," Emma went on swiftly, "the unit has the best security record in the hospital. This is the first incident since its inception, even though there are at least two or three a week on other units, all of which, presumably, follow hospital policy."

"But your system isn't authorized," he said tightly. "However successful it may be, and I'm not denying that, it goes utterly and absolutely against policy."

"I know that, but ninety-nine point nine percent of the time it works. It's part of the ethos of the unit. We couldn't have the success rate we do if we followed the rules and regulations to the letter. Most of them are totally antithetical to the ethics and philosophies of our practice, and our practice *works!*"

The tension in the room coiled, hugged them all in the lethal embrace of a boa constrictor. Delia stood frozen by the sink; Jim Lester tried to concentrate on his task, but his fingers were not as deft as they had been. Everyone knew what this would mean, and they all waited for Mark to put it into words. Before he could do so, however, there was a brisk knock at the door and a white-coated pharmacist's assistant appeared with a small package.

"Valium, I.M., ordered by Dr. Forrest," he said cheerfully, handing it to Delia as he cast an interested glance around the room.

"Thanks, Mike." She signed for it, smiled a dismissal, and handed the package to Mark, who pocketed it with a brief nod.

"You all through, Jim?"

"Just about." The last thread was cut. "It's going to hurt like the devil, Em, when the local wears off." He gave her a concerned smile.

"I know." She attempted to return the smile. "But thanks, anyway, Jim."

"Well, if you folks don't need any more surgical patching, I'll be off on my rounds." Jim got to his feet, waved a hand in general farewell, and disappeared.

"Do you want a sling, Emma?" Delia finished bandaging

the ugly wound.

Emma shook her head and glanced at Mark, who was on the phone. "Looks as if I'm going to be off my feet for a while, so it's hardly necessary."

Delia pulled a wry, sympathetic face and then turned hastily to tidy up the mess of bandages and needles lying on the counter as Mark concluded his brief instructions to Edie and replaced the phone.

"Let's go." He took Emma's good arm in a firm, supportive hold, his brisk tone indicating that her options were zero.

"Will you talk to the children?" she pleaded urgently. "It's not that I don't trust Phil and Joyce, but . . ." She shrugged helplessly.

"I'll do it," he responded with instant comprehension. "Make sure all the kids are here after school, Delia. I'll come down for a special group session at around four o'clock, and we'll put the pieces of this mess together. You also might institute a scavenger hunt for the *Policies and Procedures Manual*. It's a big red book, although I don't suppose anyone on this unit is aware of that fact!"

"Will do," Delia replied instantly, shooting Emma a slightly uneasy glance.

Emma shrugged. She couldn't do much about the manual at this point, but she needed Mark to take the children through what had just happened. They all knew and trusted him, and they still treated him, on the infrequent occasions when he managed to get to the unit, with the old familiarity and ease.

They drove home in silence. Emma had nothing more to say and knew that the next move had to come from Mark.

She tried to guess what he was thinking, noticing that he seemed quite relaxed as he drove calmly through the hectic midday traffic, but his face was set, and small frown lines had appeared between the straight eyebrows.

Apart from the fact that she felt dreadful physically as quivers of aftershock swept her body at regular intervals, her spirit was suddenly, amazingly, at ease. The moment of truth had at last come, and if she could remain firm to the end, she would have won the final battle for the unit. There would have to be an incident report, which would inevitably lead to an inquiry, and now was the time to stop ducking issues. She couldn't have won her case earlier, not until the unit was firmly established as a political necessity, but now she would tell them that if they wanted it, they would have to accept it on the only terms that made it workable. The next few days were going to be horrible, particularly for Mark, but if she could win this one, she would be winning for both of them. Once she no longer felt that they were professionally in conflict, they could become colleagues again.

Meg, who was leaving the house with her daughter Anna as they pulled up, came swiftly toward the car. "What are you two doing home at this hour? I'm just going to collect Sam from nursery school." Her eyes widened as she saw Emma's bandaged arm. "What on earth happened, Em?"

"Later, Meg," Mark replied quickly. "Emma's going to bed for the afternoon. Keep Sam away from her, will you?"

"Yes, of course," Meg replied quickly, "but what should I tell him?"

Mark leaned over, dropped a friendly, apologetic kiss on Meg's cheek. "You'll think of something, Meg."

"Sure." Meg shot a puzzled glance at Emma, who tried for a reassuring smile and failed totally, her knees buckling as she clambered out of the car. She rested against the door for a moment, and then her feet left the ground as Mark swept her up in his very strong arms.

"You're in even worse shape than I thought you were," Mark muttered, striding with her across the sidewalk and onto the porch. He stood her on her feet, holding her tightly against him, as he felt for his key, then picked her up again and carried her upstairs.

"I feel like a rag doll," Emma murmured with a shaky laugh, lying on the bed as he undressed her with swift, competent hands, flipping her over when necessary, manipulating her limbs as he drew off her clothes.

"I wish I were sure how *I* feel right now," he said shortly, filling the hypodermic syringe carefully before making a swift circular movement with his forefinger.

Sensing that protest would only exacerbate an already impossibly tense situation, Emma rolled onto her side. She felt the slight prick of the needle; then the covers were pulled up to her neck.

"That should keep you out of trouble for about four hours," Mark observed with a short laugh. "I'm going back to see what I can do to sort out this mess."

"Mark, love, *I* will sort it out," she said softly. "You have to trust me now. I admit it's going to be very uncomfortable for both of us for a while, but I know what has to be done. Trust me . . . please."

He looked down at her in frowning silence. "You really think you can pull this one out of the fire?"

"Yes." She nodded firmly, fighting the involuntary relaxation as the Valium took insidious control of her muscles. "In an odd sort of way, it was inevitable. It would have been much easier if you hadn't been on the other side of the desk when it happened, but you are and there's nothing either of us can do about it." Her eyelids drooped, and she felt his lips on hers.

"You are the most amazing creature, my sweet Emma," he whispered on a soft laugh. "You've always got something up your sleeve, and I suppose I'm going to have to ride along with you on this one, as always. It's curiously exciting, but excessively exhausting!"

She felt his lips curve against hers, but couldn't have spoken if her life depended on it.

It seemed only the next instant that the clatter of cups and the sigh of the mattress as it yielded to Mark's weight brought her back into lethargic wakefulness.

"Tea?" His smiling face hung mistily above her, and she pushed the mist away, returned the smile.

"No sugar this time?"

"Not a grain."

She struggled up against the pillows, wincing at the deep, tight ache in her injured arm, and reached for the cup.

"What's that you're drinking?" She frowned at his glass.

"Scotch." He grinned. "I'm not full of Valium, and I've had one hell of an afternoon!"

"Tell me the worst," Emma sighed, sipping the fragrant, revivifying liquid, trying to ignore the pain in her arm.

"An inquiry, as I imagine you realized," he stated succinctly.

"Not headed by you." It was a statement, not a question.

"I've declared a conflict of interest. Charles Graves will

take the chair."

"You talked to him?"

"I did."

"What did he say?"

"It doesn't bear repeating, Emma mine."

"Uh-oh!" She grimaced. "I can't fight this one without Charles on my side."

"He *is* on your side, just as I am. We both had the same initial reaction, that's all."

"I won't ask you what that was," she said wryly.

"It was very chauvinistic," Mark responded blandly, refilling her cup.

Emma decided it would be wise not to pursue that particular conversational avenue. "When's the inquiry?"

"Next Friday. Charles suggested you take sick leave until then," he said casually.

"As an alternative to suspension?" she queried, feeling her hackles rise.

"Sweet, you are in big trouble, whether or not you believe you can get out of it. If they want to throw the book at you on this one, they can."

"They won't," Emma responded with calm confidence. "I know exactly how I'm going to play it. I'm going to attack! It's high time I issued an ultimatum, and now I'm ready to put the whole thing on the line. In a strange sort of way, I feel I have nothing to lose anymore," she added thoughtfully.

Mark regarded her closely. "Because of our situation?"

"Maybe," she said with deliberate vagueness, "but I think it has more to do with the fact that your becoming medical director has acted as a catalyst for me. I couldn't go on in the way I have been. It's too much of a strain, particularly with all the new calls on my time." She gave him an oblique look that brought a curve to the full mouth. "However, my darling," she continued with brisk resolution, "I'm afraid you're going to have to be at that inquiry. Not in the chair, of course, but as medical director, you have to hear my spiel."

"Can I hear it beforehand?"

"Sure," she responded easily. "But I'm not going to take a sick leave. That would be an implicit admission of guilt, and I have been guilty of nothing but ensuring the success that everyone wants and *needs*. If the board members don't like my methods, then they can look elsewhere for someone to run the unit. If they want to suspend me, they can do so."

"This has really got your fighting spirit up," Mark remarked, dropping a large red book on her lap with a casual gesture.

"Oh, you found it!" she exclaimed, frowning wryly at the somewhat grubby state of what should have been a pristine copy of the declaration and description of every aspect of life on the kids' unit.

"*I* didn't," he responded dryly. "The kids did. The thought that you might be out of a job if this manual wasn't found by the close of business today worked wonders!"

"You *didn't!*" she said, shocked.

"Oh, yes, I did, Emma mine, and I almost meant it!" He was laughing, but there was a gravity behind the humor.

"Where was it?" she asked, not sure she really wanted to know.

"Nestling among the dust balls behind Timmy's dresser,"

he said coolly. "Apparently, you gave it to him months ago to use as a lap table while drawing pictures in bed."

"Did I really?" Emma's eyes widened in mock horror. It was considered a sacrilege to allow a patient to see the *Policies and Procedures Manual*; never mind that Timmy Baldwin was only five years old and his reading hadn't progressed beyond the "cat sat on the mat" stage!

Mark grinned at her. "Appalling woman! I cannot imagine how such a calm, easygoing individual found himself married to such a rebellious dynamo!"

"So that's how you would describe yourself?" She returned his grin over the rim of her cup.

"That's exactly how I would describe myself, and you can stop looking at me with those enormous, lustful eyes, Emma mine. It's not going to get you anywhere! I know exactly how that arm of yours feels."

"What a pity," she sighed, pushing aside the bedcovers with the arm that wasn't throbbing. "In that case, I'd better go do my maternal duty. I hear my son's eager tones."

"You will remain in that bed until I give you permission to leave it." Mark replaced the covers and got to his feet. "Sam can visit with you for half an hour. You can eat dinner together, and then you'll take a painkiller and go back to sleep. Do I make myself understood, wife?"

"Clear as a bell, husband," she trilled, subsiding with considerable relief against the pillows at her back. "We'll get through this, Mark." Her voice carried total conviction, and he smiled down at her.

"I don't doubt it, sweet. One of these days, we might even reach a plateau."

"Oh, I hope not," she declared fervently.

"So do I! Living and working with you, my love, is about the most exciting, entrancing, exhilarating experience I could ever have imagined; also the most exhausting," he teased.

"It's got to be boring sometimes," she murmured.

"Never! But just once in a while, you might try to behave yourself." He nipped the tip of her nose, and she wriggled. "Just so that, occasionally, I can pretend I married an ordinary woman."

"I *am* an ordinary woman." Emma's eyes danced.

"You are a soft, sweet, magical bundle who can turn into the most devastating professional dynamo at the drop of a hat," he replied. "I love you both, Dr. Grantham and Mrs. Forrest."

"Then kiss us both," she whispered.

"You can go in now, Dr. Grantham." The secretary put down the telephone and smiled sympathetically as Emma squared her shoulders, picked up the stack of papers, and walked, with a calm self-possession that she didn't feel, into the boardroom the following Friday. It was a rather different atmosphere from the last time she'd been here. An empty chair for the "accused" stood in lonely isolation at the end of the long table facing a very somber Charles Graves.

"Good morning, Dr. Grantham," he said formally. "Please sit down."

"Thank you. Good morning," she replied politely, taking her seat as she glanced briefly at the sea of serious faces. She didn't want to look at Mark, but couldn't help herself. His posture indicated relaxation, but his face was set, and she knew that he was not relaxed at all. He was suffering agonies of embarrassment, and her heart yearned toward him empathetically. For his sake, almost more than for her own and the children's, she had to pull this one off. She wasn't going to escape unscathed—she was under no illusions on that score, knowing that the board couldn't allow this dereliction to pass unmarked—but if she could get them to accept her justification and her new proposal, she would have won a major victory.

"We are inquiring, Dr. Grantham, into the incident that took place on the children's unit last Friday," Charles began.

Emma inclined her head but said nothing. She was not about to rush into explanations; let them speak first.

"We have all read your incident report," he continued when it was clear that she was not about to take the initiative. "I should say, at this point, that we commend your swift action to avert a major disaster."

She inclined her head in brief acknowledgment again.

"However, we are very disturbed by the fact that the children involved were not screened by our security guards when they returned to the building, as is mandatory under hospital policy and state regulations. That is correct, is it not?"

"It is," she replied calmly.

"Is it also correct, Dr. Grantham, that for the last two and a half years you have taken total responsibility for security checks on the children's unit?"

"It is," she said again.

There was a short silence and a glint of humor appeared in Charles's gray eyes. "Do you perhaps have an explanation, Dr. Grantham?" he asked gently.

Emma opened the folder in front of her, felt in the pocket of her linen jacket for her glasses, and looked with brisk confidence around the table. "I think it will be simpler if I just pass out some material. These are copies of three incident reports I made two and a half years ago. They describe the humiliations three of our children were subjected to during a routine security check. As a result of these incidents, I wrote a formal complaint to the head of security. Here are copies of my complaint and his reply. I am sure you will all find his explanation as unsatisfactory as I did."

She sat quietly as they read the material. Then Charles looked up. "Did you discuss this with the medical director at the time?"

"I did, and I also told him that I would take certain measures to ensure that this did not happen again. He did not ask me to describe those measures."

Charles's lips twitched. "On the principle that ignorance is bliss, I assume?"

Emma lowered her eyes to hide her own responding gleam. That was exactly the way Felix had operated when it came to the kids' unit.

"Surely the security department was aware of your changed system?" a voice broke in somewhere on her left.

"You'd certainly think they'd have noticed, Mr. Johnson," Emma agreed smoothly. "I didn't, however, notify them myself, and there's a very rapid staff turnover in that department. Since they work a shift system with little communication at changeover, I don't think anyone realized that the children on the unit were never being checked in, particularly as I didn't inform security when the kids left on pass. The unit is considered to be something of a mystery within many departments of the hospital, anyway. Anyone who did notice would probably just assume it was one of those peculiarities of our operation."

"What you are saying, I think, Dr. Grantham, is that you have used the faults inherent in a large bureaucratic system to get around that system?" Charles examined her thoughtfully, that same glint of humor in his eyes.

"You could put it that way," she murmured. She had nothing to lose at this point by admitting the full extent of her dereliction.

There was a moment of reflective silence in the room, which, eventually, Emma broke. "I also have some statistics on the number of incidents in the last month on other units in the hospital. They all relate to the smuggling in of forbidden objects. I am assuming that the usual security checks took place in every case. Last Friday's incident, while it was regrettable, was the first of its kind on the unit since we started operating our own system." She passed out the papers and waited.

"Looks as if we need a total overhaul of security, Mark," Charles remarked thoughtfully.

Mark nodded. "It's at the head of my agenda."

Charles turned back to Emma. "This is all very convincing, Dr. Grantham, but the fact remains that the unit is out of compliance with a fundamental hospital regulation. We are obliged to abide by state regulations when it comes to security, however unsatisfactory the system."

"I have a compromise proposal," Emma said calmly. "If we must use the security system on the unit, then I would like to take two members of that department onto the unit team and train them in our methods and philosophies; they would work exclusively with the children, under my supervision. That, I think, should satisfy everyone."

"Except, perhaps, the head of security," Charles observed.

Emma met his gaze steadily. "That is neither my problem nor my concern. The children *are* my concern as is the continuing success of the unit. I cannot guarantee that success if we're obliged to abide by rules that are both ineffectual and damaging to our operation."

There. Finally she had said it. She had just issued an ultimatum and her job and the continuation of the unit now hung on the board's reaction. She cast a quick glance at Mark. His face was impassive, but then, he had been prepared for her remarks. Before the inquiry, she had explained to him in great detail everything she intended to say.

"Would you mind waiting outside, Dr. Grantham?" Charles asked quietly. "The board must now discuss what action to take in this matter."

Emma rose immediately as Charles turned courteously toward Mark. "This must be very uncomfortable for you, Dr. Forrest. If you would prefer not to stay for our deliberations, we'll understand."

Mark shook his head. "That's very considerate of you, Mr. Graves, but I will remain, although I would much rather not take an active part in your decision."

"Of course." Charles turned back to Emma. "We won't keep you long, Dr. Grantham."

Emma went into the anteroom, curiously calm. Her main concern at this point was for Mark. He was going to have to sit there listening while they decided her fate. Somehow, she had to make sure he was never put in this position again.

A sudden burst of laughter from behind the closed door brought her eyebrows up. She glanced questioningly at the secretary.

"Sounds like you're off the hook, Em." The woman grinned. "I've never heard them laugh when they're about to send someone to the gallows." Her intercom buzzer sounded, and she picked up the phone. She listened for a few seconds, then jerked her head toward the door. "You're on, Em. Good luck!"

"Thanks." Emma smiled and walked into the boardroom. The atmosphere there had changed; the earlier gravity and tension had dissipated. Mark was leaning back in his chair, hands thrust deep into his pockets, a wide grin on his face. He dropped one eyelid in an almost imperceptible wink as she took her seat, and she relaxed.

"As I'm sure you realize, Dr. Grantham, we are obliged to take some form of disciplinary action," Graves began formally, although his eyes twinkled. "The unit has been flagrantly out of compliance with a fundamental regulation for several years—a fact that you have admitted quite openly. We cannot institute an inquiry and then ignore the findings of the inquiry."

"Of course not," Emma concurred smoothly. She knew now that she was home free and would endure the bureaucratic formalities with as much grace as she could muster.

"We were sure you would see it our way," Graves murmured, as another ripple of amusement ran around the table. "You may consider that you have received a private, unrecorded reprimand, Emma. It's the least we can do."

Emma's smile met his and those of the others around the table.

"Now, as far as this proposal is concerned." Charles tapped the paper on the table in front of him. "I suggest you implement it as soon as possible. You have the board's unconditional approval."

Jubilation washed through her. She'd done it!

"One further suggestion," he continued smoothly. "If, as I strongly suspect, there are other areas on the unit where you are totally out of compliance, any imaginative proposals that you can come up with to ensure a satisfactory compromise will enjoy a favorable reception. You will, of course, work through the medical director in this matter."

Emma nodded, glancing at Mark. They were already nearly finished, having spent the last few days with the unit's *Policies and Procedures Manual*. He winked at her again.

"Thank heaven that's over," Charles said with a sigh of relief. "I don't remember spending a more uncomfortable morning!"

"You and me both, Charles," Mark declared, getting to his feet. "If you'll all excuse us, I'm going to take Dr. Grantham out for lunch."

"That must have been horrible for you," Emma whispered, as they stood in the elevator.

"Appalling," he concurred, "but you were magnificent."

"It won't ever happen again," she promised, taking his hand.

"I find that hard to believe, Emma mine." Mark smiled. "Just keep me in the picture as much as you can—okay?"

"I am going to make sure that it *never* happens again," she reiterated firmly.

11

"ABOUT EIGHT WEEKS, I would say, Emma." Neil Carter dried his hands vigorously on a paper towel as she slipped off the examining table in his office. "We'll do a pregnancy test, just for the record, but I don't think there's any doubt about the result."

"Not the way I feel, these mornings, Neil," Emma said ruefully.

"It'll pass." He smiled. "You were the same with Sam."

"I remember *now*." She grimaced. "Mother Nature's very sneaky when it comes to perpetuating the human race. There's a total memory blank on the more unpleasant side effects."

He laughed. "I bet Mark's in seventh heaven."

"He doesn't know yet. It's my turn to produce the surprise this time." Emma chuckled softly. "You won't mention it at the Rosens' tonight, will you?"

"My lips are sealed," he promised. "If you follow the same pattern as last time, you'll be able to keep him in the dark for six months. I thought you were going to deliver a mouse, instead of seven pounds of vociferous little boy!"

"I'm built funny." She laughed. "But I'm not going to keep it a secret for more than a couple of days."

"Come into the office when you're dressed, and we'll

discuss practicalities."

Emma drove back to St. Anne's in a soft glow of pleasure. She hadn't needed Neil's confirmation of her pregnancy, had actually known it for the last four weeks. The queasiness had started the morning of the inquiry, but on that day it could have been caused by any number of things! However, she had been hitting the bathroom every morning since, as soon as her eyes opened. So far, Mark had not appeared to notice, and she hugged her secret in covert delight. This was one present he was going to love.

Back in her office, she pulled the memo pad toward her, frowned, then with a quick grin scribbled rapidly. That should do it! She tucked the request for a three month leave of absence beginning in January into an envelope marked "personal," addressed it to the medical director, and dropped it into the internal mail basket.

"You feeling all right, Em?" Delia inquired casually as Emma walked into the nurses' station an hour later, munching hungrily on a very large cheeseburger dripping onions and ketchup.

"Sure," she responded. "Why?"

"You look a bit pale," Delia replied with a shrug, "and if you're not in the bathroom these days, you're eating."

Emma took another bite, tore off a paper towel to wipe the sticky mess from her fingers. "Odd, isn't it?" she commented.

"Very," Delia agreed gravely. "When's it due?"

"End of January." Emma gave a small skip of pleasure. "You're not to breathe a word to anyone, Delia."

"Why the secrecy?" Delia grinned.

"I haven't told Mark yet. I can't understand why he hasn't guessed. I had exactly this conversation with Meg three days ago."

"Women," Delia explained sagely.

"I guess that's it."

"Bye, love, see you tonight." Emma kissed the top of Mark's head on her way out of the kitchen the next morning.

He looked up absently from the newspaper, smiled that special, remembering smile that made last night so incredibly vivid again, and patted her bottom in his usual fashion. "Don't be late, Emma mine."

"As if I would!" she said scornfully, and went out to her car.

She rather suspected that she would be seeing him before tonight. Her request for a leave of absence should be on his desk this morning, and she couldn't imagine that he would wait until the evening for an explanation. But the voice on the other end of the phone when he called her midmorning bore no relation to her secret, pleasurable imaginings.

"Get up here, Emma!" He sounded furious, and her heart jumped painfully.

"What's the matter, love?"

"If you're not up here in five minutes, I'll come and get you. If you want to make this a public affair, that's fine by me!" The line went dead, and Emma gulped. What on earth was wrong? But she certainly wasn't prepared to find out in public, and Mark never made idle threats. Not that he was actually in the habit of making threats, she reflected, hurrying through the corridors.

The red light shone over Mark's closed door when she entered Edie's office. "Go right in, Dr. Grantham." For once, Edie offered no obstruction.

Mark swung around from the window as she entered. "Close the door!" His eyes were brown stones set in a rigid white face.

"What is it?" Her heart began to thump, her palms to moisten. She'd never imagined he could look like this.

"What the hell do you mean, what is it?" he said furiously.

"It's this, of course!" Her memo fluttered under her nose, and she took an involuntary step backward, away from that livid face. "Just what are you trying to do?"

"But . . . but it's just a request for a leave of absence," she stammered. "You *are* the right person to address it to, aren't you?"

"Don't you play games with me, Emma Grantham," he said dangerously. "You don't really think I'm going to let you do this, do you?"

Emma looked at him, speechless with confusion. Something had backfired explosively, and she still wasn't sure what, how, or why.

"You really think running away is going to solve anything?" He was gripping her shoulders, and she had an uneasy feeling he was about to shake her.

"I don't understand," she said desperately. "Run away from what?"

"Is this your idea of a joke?" he hissed, his fingers tightening.

"No . . . no, of course it isn't," she cried. "Oh, please calm down and tell me exactly what's bothering you."

"After the inquiry, you said you were going to ensure that we were never put in such a position again," he said tightly. "If leaving the hospital is your idea of a solution, I'm telling you once and for all that you can forget it!"

At last the pieces fell into place. Quite clearly, he had not read her request carefully.

"Look at my request again, Mark," Emma said quietly. "If I'd had such a cockeyed idea, do you really think I'd ask for a leave seven months from now? I'd want it immediately."

"What?" He released her with a frown, reread the mangled piece of paper in his hands.

"January!" he exclaimed. "What the hell's going on, Emma?"

"It's usually called maternity leave," she said softly.

His face expressed total incredulity. "Are you telling me you're pregnant?"

She nodded silently.

"How?" he demanded.

"You mean there's more than one way?" Emma tried unsuccessfully for a light tone.

Mark just looked at her, and her tentative smile died. Oh, how could such a happy scheme go so far awry? How could she ever have made such a mistake?

"Why didn't you tell me?" He spoke very quietly now.

"I wanted it to be a surprise," she said miserably. "You know you like surprises. I thought this would be the best one ever. You've always said it was up to me to decide when, or even if, we were to have a baby, but I knew you wanted one. You do, don't you?"

"Yes, of course I do," Mark stated flatly. "I would like to

have known what was up, that's all."

Tears pricked behind her eyes, and she turned hastily away from him. "I'm sorry . . . I made a mistake. I thought I should wait until I actually got pregnant and then . . . oh, I only wanted to please you!"

The next instant her head was buried against his chest and his hands were stroking the back of her neck as he kissed the cornsilk crown of her hair. "Oh, my sweet Emma, you have. I'm so sorry, darling. All I saw was the request for leave, and after what we've been through just recently and what you said, I jumped to conclusions in a red mist of fury. Look at me . . . please." His strong fingers lifted her chin. "Don't cry, sweet. How could I have been such an insensitive brute?" He pulled her over to the couch and sat down, drawing her onto his lap.

"Pregnant women tend to cry a lot," she mumbled with a sniff as he wiped her eyes with his handkerchief.

"Blow," he instructed on a somewhat watery chuckle of his own, holding the handkerchief to her nose.

Emma obeyed, then settled with a sigh into his arms.

"Have you seen Neil?" Mark stroked her cheeks with a delicate fingertip.

"Yesterday," she replied. "It's quite official."

"I've been very blind," he mused, unbuttoning her shirt, sliding a hand around to unhook her bra. "You've been spending so much time in the bathroom recently, particularly first thing in the morning. I'd noticed, but somehow it didn't really register; mornings are such chaos anyway." His fingers began to play over her breasts as he released them from the confining bra. "I've been wondering whether I was imagining that your breasts were larger," he remarked, laughing softly. "What a fool!"

"Well, you didn't know I was planning a surprise," she murmured, stretching contentedly under his fingers. "I'm sorry about that. I didn't realize you'd be so upset about not knowing."

"Ordinarily, I wouldn't have been," he said his lips brushing the corner of her mouth gently. "I was so furious with you already—that was the trouble."

"I don't know how you could have imagined I would abandon the unit," she said with an attempt at severity.

"Neither do I. Forgive me?" His eyes smiled down at her, glowing with the warm light of love, and she reached up to capture his lips.

"Oh, Lord," he muttered, crushing her to him with an almost convulsive fierceness. "I need you so!"

"And I you," she whispered against his mouth, pressing herself into his body as if, in some way, she could melt her flesh into his.

He raised his head, breathing raggedly. "Isn't Sam spending the afternoon with a friend?"

"Yes. I'll pick him up on my way home, around six. Why?"

"We're going home now," he declared firmly. "We'll get some retsina. Then we'll stop at the Greek deli to pick up a little taramas, a few black olives, and pita bread, and have a feast in bed."

"Are you suggesting we play hooky, Mr. Medical Director?" Emma grinned. "Shame on you! What sort of an example is that to set?"

"I don't give a damn," he announced cheerfully. "Come on, now, up!" The instruction was accompanied by another of his brisk pats.

"That particular habit, Mark Forrest, you are going to have to drop," she said firmly, fumbling behind her to fasten her bra. "It's no way to treat a pregnant lady."

"Oh?" He laughed, turning her around, deftly fastening the hooks, his hands lingering on the warm skin of her back. "And how should a pregnant lady be treated?"

"With respect," she pronounced in dignified accents.

"Like this?" One hand insinuated itself inside the waistband of her skirt as the other undid the button and zipper.

"Mark!" she exclaimed on a choke of laughter as her skirt fell to her ankles and his fingers slid inside her pantyhose to smooth a gentle seductive caress over her stomach. "What happens if Edie comes in?"

"I have a feeling she's going to find me making love to my wife," he whispered unevenly, a husky throb in his mellow voice.

"Surely not on the desk?" she murmured as that wonderful excitement created by the knowing touch of his fingers took possession of her.

"The couch." He pulled her backward, and she fell with a soft moan onto the nubby, slightly prickly upholstery.

"Mark, this is crazy!" But she couldn't translate her verbal protest into action as he swiftly drew off her pantyhose, and she lay, naked except for her shirt and bra, on the couch in the office of St. Anne's chief-administrator in the middle of a Thursday morning.

"I've always wanted to do this," he growled with a low, sensual chuckle. "Nobody's going to come in without warning, anyway." He began taking off his own clothes, and gales of muted laughter swooped through her.

"What if there's a fire?" she gasped, opening her arms to him as he dropped gently on top of her.

"Quiet, or you'll have a negative effect!" he instructed, trying to control his own laughter. Then they were joined, and passion chased away their mirth in a glorious tide of renewal that blocked out all thoughts of their surroundings; every alarm bell in the hospital could have gone off, but that would have made no difference to them as their urgent, insistent bodies clamored for each other, expressing an almost febrile need as the world shattered, sparked around them in a myriad of tiny pieces that, as miraculously as always, fell back into place again—a perfect picture.

"Oh, darling," Emma whispered against his shoulder. There were no other words, even if she could have articulated them at this moment.

"It's always so wonderful, and it's always so different," he murmured, kissing her eyelids tenderly. "But I can't help feeling we've pushed our luck far enough for one day!" Laughter again danced in his brown eyes as he struggled upright, reaching for his clothes.

"We are very wicked," Emma announced smugly, pulling on her pantyhose. "Where's my skirt?"

"Over there." He grinned, pointing to the middle of the room. "We must have been out of our minds!"

"*You* were," she emphasized playfully, zipping up her skirt. "I did try to point out the various eventualities, if you remember?"

"I was beyond reason," he agreed smoothly. "Hurry up and get your things together, Emma mine. That merely whetted my appetite; I now need a three-course meal!"

"Greedy," she teased, making for the door. "Oh, by the

way"—mockery lurked in her dulcet tones—"can I assume that my request for leave has been approved?"

"When I receive an official, typed request for maternity leave, as opposed to this confusing scrawl, you may do so," Mark responded smartly.

"Pompous bureaucrat!" Emma whisked herself out of the office, closing the door firmly as he lunged toward it. Smiling sweetly at Edie, she danced her way to her office.

12

"THIS IS NO GOOD!" Emma struggled in frustration with the waistband of her skirt. "I can't find a safety pin big enough anymore!"

"Perhaps it's time to buy yourself some expandable clothes." Mark's calm voice was muffled as he pulled a thick sweater over his head.

"Maternity clothes?" She wrinkled her nose distastefully, turning sideways to the mirror, grimacing at her image.

"It's customary," he observed, bending to tie the laces of his sneakers.

"But then I'd *really* look pregnant."

"Emma, sweet, you *are* pregnant." He stood up slowly, regarding her gravely. "Six months pregnant, to be precise.

"Yes, but once I go in for the whole show, I'll have to be aware of it," she explained with a sigh. "I hate being pregnant. The waiting is so awful, and the longer I can go on pretending the better."

"You can't go on pretending any longer," Mark declared crisply, coming toward her, taking her shoulders firmly. He had that determined look about him, and Emma's heart sank a little. He was obviously going to be bossy again. "It's time you and I had a little chat, Emma mine."

"Why do I feel that *you* are going to be doing all the chatting, and that I'm not going to enjoy the listening?" she grumbled as he drew her toward the bed.

"Probably because you're getting used to me," he said evenly. "Sit down."

"I think I'd rather stand," she muttered, but sat nevertheless.

"I had really hoped to avoid this," Mark began, "but you're reducing my options rather rapidly, my love."

"Get it over with," Emma sighed.

"Neil called me at the beginning of the week."

"Why would he want to do that?" she protested indignantly.

"Because he felt there were certain things I ought to know, and he made the remarkably accurate assumption that you wouldn't tell them to me yourself," was the uncomfortable response.

Emma didn't need to ask what things Neil thought Mark ought to know. "Neil's just a worrywart," she retorted.

"I think not," Mark replied. "Your blood pressure is up, and you're not gaining any weight," he went on levelly.

"My blood pressure is *not* high!" She started to rise from the bed and then, catching his eye, decided against it. "It's always a bit lower than normal, so now it's about as high as the average person's."

"It's high for you," he stated uncompromisingly. "Neil is *not* happy about it. He told me he had made various suggestions last month as to how you might change your lifestyle. You haven't taken his advice, and I'm tired of waiting for you to make some minimal adjustments to accommodate what is rapidly becoming an advanced state of pregnancy!"

"What are you saying, Mark?" She sighed.

"I am saying, Emma, that you have to get your blood pressure on an even keel very fast, and you *must* gain some weight."

"I don't want to gain weight," she protested. "I'm fat enough already, and it's terribly hard to lose afterward. I don't want to roll around like a doughnut for months!"

"Sweet, that baby is going to take everything it needs from you." Mark was making a visible effort to sound reasonable. "In the end, you'll both suffer if you go on like this."

"You're right, of course." Lacking a single weapon in her arsenal, Emma gave up the fight. "I'll try to get more rest." She got up as if to signal that the subject was closed.

"Emma," Mark began carefully, "I don't think you quite understand. You no longer have the option to try. You *will*."

"Will?" She stared at him.

"Yes, *will*," he repeated. "You will work from nine to five instead of this insane seven-thirty in the morning to six-thirty in the evening routine. You will take an hour for lunch away from your desk, and you will eat three sensible meals a day. No more of this grabbing an apple in the morning and running through the halls with a half-eaten sandwich at lunchtime. And, finally, my love, you will be in bed, or at least resting with your feet up, by ten o'clock every weekday evening."

"Mark!" she exclaimed as a surge of annoyance washed through her. "I'm pregnant; I'm not an invalid!"

"The regimen I have just described is practiced by the majority of the thinking, working, population even when they are not adding extra burdens to their system," he retorted.

Emma looked at him for a moment, and then shrugged. "Okay, I said I would try, and I will *try*."

Mark ran a weary hand over his eyes and sighed heavily. "I didn't want it to come to this, but if you are not prepared to follow Neil's orders to the letter—and they are doctor's orders, make no mistake about that—I'll put you on administrative leave for the next three months."

Emma's jaw dropped. "You wouldn't . . . ? You couldn't!" she gasped.

"I can and I will," he responded quietly.

"On what grounds?" she demanded, unable to believe she was hearing this.

"Medical grounds. Neil will send me a letter saying that working with your elevated blood pressure is, to use the buzzword, contraindicated," he stated bluntly.

"You cooked that up between you!" She gazed at him in total disbelief.

"We had to come up with something as a last resort."

"What right do you have?" she demanded and saw, for the first time in this entire conversation, a flash of anger in his eyes.

"I have a fistful of rights where you're concerned," he said tightly, "and do you want to know why? Because I love you, because you are a part of me. I am no more prepared to watch you embark on a mission of self-destruction than I would be to watch myself. If I have to do the equivalent of putting a lock on Sam's window to prevent him endangering himself on the porch roof, then so be it!"

Emma swallowed. She couldn't deal with any of this right now. "I have to go out for awhile," she said slowly and without waiting for his response, left the bedroom.

Sam catapulted across the hall as she reached for her purse in the closet. "You goin' out, Mommy?" he shrilled. "Can I come? It's Satday!"

Emma bent to kiss him. "I know it is, darling, but I have some errands to do by myself. Mark's upstairs, though. Why don't you go see what plans he's got? You know he's always full of good ideas."

The little boy looked disappointed for a minute and then suddenly beamed. "Mark said he'd fix my swing today. We have to go buy some more rope." With that, he turned and hurtled up the stairs, yelling for Mark.

Emma smiled and went to the bee. That had been a singularly uncomfortable half-hour, and all the more so because she had been totally in the wrong! If Mark was being authoritarian, it was because she had driven him to it. It was not in his nature to lay down the law. Even in his role as medical director, he managed always to give the impression that he was asking favors of people rather than giving orders—not that anybody ever denied him the favor!

She drove thoughtfully into Boston, only absently noticing the glory of the New England fall. It was so very difficult to break the habits of a lifetime. She had never coddled herself, had always worked until she dropped, and had never permitted anyone to dictate to her in the way she ran her life. And now there was someone in her life who was saying not only that he didn't like what she was doing but that he had the right to insist that she change. She was willing to admit that she had not been behaving in a particularly sensible fashion recently, and however much she might deny it, her body was giving her unmistakable messages. But did Mark have the *right* to insist that she change?

Frowning, she found a parking space in the Prudential Center and, in response to the grumbling of her stomach, went in search of breakfast. She might as well start following doctor's orders immediately. It took her a plate of scrambled eggs and two cups of coffee to decide that her husband did have the love-given right to protect her, even if she didn't think she wanted it. And it was a right that worked both ways. She would fight Mark tooth and nail if she thought he was unknowingly on a course of self-destruction, and she'd do it because she loved him. A soft glow transfused her. They actually *did* belong to each other. In spite of their separateness, they had duties and obligations toward each other and Mark had merely been exercising his and demanding that she exercise hers in her turn.

This marriage business seemed to be a never-ending learning experience, Emma reflected, as she paid the check and marched determinedly into Saks.

It was three hours later when she pulled up outside the house, the back seat of her car piled high with boxes and shopping bags. Deciding to leave them there for the moment, she went up on the porch. Sam's eager, excited shouts reached her, coming from the back yard, and she turned toward the side gate, opening it quietly.

They were raking leaves, or at least Mark was; Sam

seemed to be rushing up and down the garden with his wheelbarrow, scattering the tidy piles to the four winds again! Mark appeared totally unperturbed, his tall, broad figure, clad in jeans and a heavy, cable-knit sweater, swinging rhythmically with the rake.

Sam saw her first and, with his usual repetitive shout— "It's Mommy, Mark! Mommy's back, Mark!"—hurled himself at her. She lifted him with rather less than her usual ease—one of them was getting heavy, these days!—and he perched on her hip, the chubby legs having some difficulty getting a hold around the roundness of her belly.

Mark turned toward her, resting on the rake. His eyes were grave, appraising, but he smiled somewhat quizzically.

"Looks as if you two have been busy," she said cheerfully, crossing the grass, her feet rustling through the tawny-gold carpet.

"Busy certainly," he said laughingly as she reached him. "How productive, I'm not so sure."

She lifted her face, and he bent to kiss her gently. "How about you, Emma mine?"

"Both busy and productive," she declared. "I need help unloading the car."

"Have you had lunch?" The gravity was still in his eyes.

"No." She shook her head. "But I did have an enormous breakfast."

"Mark made pasta for lunch," Sam yelled at his usual volume. "We saved some for you."

Emma rubbed her ear, pretending it hurt from his shout. "I'm not on the other side of the fence, sweetheart!"

Mark took Sam out of her arms firmly. "You're getting

heavy, young man. Let's go unload the bee, and then we'll get Mommy's lunch."

"Oh, it's okay, I'll just grab a . . ." Her unthinking protestation died. "I love pasta," she amended.

Laughter sprang in Mark's eyes, chasing away the serious, questioning look. "That's fortunate, since we saved you a lot!"

"Wass all that?" Sam demanded as they opened the back door of the car. "Are they s'prises?"

"Dear Lord," Mark murmured, "did you buy up the entire store?"

"Almost." She grinned, handing out parcels. "Can you manage these, Sam?"

Sam nodded importantly, and she loaded his outstretched arms. "Is there a s'prise for me?" He stomped up the porch steps.

"There's a surprise for everyone," Emma declared cheerfully. "Put them on the kitchen table and I'll show you. I've had a fun morning!"

She opened the packages, hindered rather than helped by Sam's eager little fingers, and watched Mark's face as the pile of baby clothes, crib blankets, receiving blankets, and tiny flowered sheets grew on the kitchen table. He looked first stunned, then delighted, then awed as he fingered them.

"They're so tiny!"

"Babies do tend to be at first," she said seriously, hiding her smile. "Sam, this is for you." She handed him a gift-wrapped box.

"Thass all for the baby?" he demanded in an amazingly quiet tone, clutching his present tightly.

"Well, the baby didn't have anything at all," she explained quietly. "They're birthday presents, but it's not your birthday yet."

Sam frowned, absorbing this, then suddenly nodded as if he found that explanation entirely satisfactory and turned to his own present, tearing off the pretty wrapping paper with hasty, excited fingers. "A Lego jeep!" he shrieked. "I been wantin' one of them."

"I know you have." Emma smiled. "Why don't you go put it together in your room?"

"Awright," he announced. "Gonna build a garage for it, too."

Mark laughed, watching the boy's somewhat tempestuous departure. "You handled that one all right," he commented. "I don't think he's going to have too much of a problem when the time comes."

"No, neither do I," she agreed. "Now, *this* is for you, husband." Grinning broadly, she held out a large, flat box.

"I've just had the best present you could have given me," he responded, before opening the box.

"Do you like it? Put it on." Emma pranced eagerly around him.

"It's beautiful." Mark pulled the soft russet-colored cashmere sweater from its tissue paper and held it up.

"It's exactly the right color," Emma pronounced with satisfaction. "It matches your eyes perfectly. Put it on."

Laughing, Mark complied, stripping to the waist, folding his cable-knit sweater carefully, and placing it on a chair.

Emma drew in her breath, melting as she looked at the broad chest, the strong arms that were just for her. He caught her look and paused in the act of pulling the new sweater over his head. Glints of mischief danced in his eyes. "There's a charge for this striptease!"

"I'll pay anything," she murmured seductively.

"Anything?" he drawled lazily.

"Without reason," she returned absolutely. "You are beyond price."

"Then it's very fortunate that you *don't* have to pay for me." Mark grinned, thrusting his arms into the sleeves of the sweater. "I'd hate to price myself out of the market! Now, I'd like to know what you bought for yourself."

"Clothes—lots and lots of them," Emma informed him casually. "Clothes to work in, to play in, to dance in—but not to sleep in," she added, giving him one of her coy looks. His eyes gleamed responsively. "It does seem extravagant, though," Emma mused, "just for three months."

"You could always use them next time."

Her eyebrows disappeared into her scalp, and he grinned again, flicking her chin lightly with a fingertip.

"Perhaps that's not such a brilliant idea! I'm not sure I've got the stamina to go through this again."

"I'm sorry," Emma said quietly, burying her face in his chest. "You've the right and always will."

Strong fingers grasped the back of her neck and squeezed in firm reassurance and relief.

"Do you think since it's both New Year's Eve and our wedding anniversary that I might have an extension tonight?" Emma bent as far as she was able toward the dresser mirror, wielding her eyeliner, her lips curved in a broad, mischievous smile.

"Until midnight, Cinderella," Mark laughed, looking up from his frowning concentration on his cuff links. "After that, the coach turns into a pumpkin."

"And I get to go home with the prince," she murmured contentedly.

Mark came to stand behind her, warm tenderness glowing in his eyes as he put his arms around her, stroked the fullness of her breasts, the hard swell of her belly. His hand jumped involuntarily, and they both laughed. "That particular pumpkin is very active tonight," he observed. "And you, my darling, look utterly beautiful."

"Actually, I *feel* beautiful." Emma smiled. It was true. Since she had been . . . persuaded . . . to change her lifestyle, she had begun to feel better than she could ever remember. Her skin glowed with a radiant translucence, and her eyes shone with the clear sparkle of contentment and health. She had even come to terms with her body, finding satisfaction in its ripe, burgeoning fertility. But then, it would be hard not to when Mark made no secret of how alluring he found her, and when their lovemaking took them to such incredible heights of shared tenderness and wonder.

"Give me your left hand," he said softly. "I haven't given you your anniversary gift yet."

Reaching into his pocket, he drew out a small box and, as she watched in fascination, slipped a perfect pearl in a platinum setting onto her ring finger.

"Oh, darling, it's gorgeous," she breathed, holding out her hand, examining the pearly opalescence under the light.

"It seemed appropriate, somehow." Mark smiled. "I

know we agreed not to wear wedding bands, and I won't mind if you want to wear it on the other hand."

She shook her head. "I like it on this finger. But this is really funny, my love." Her eyes danced as she reached into a dresser drawer and took out another small box. "I wanted to give you this, but you don't have to wear it. Just keep it."

Mark opened the box and gave a soft, delighted chuckle as he took out the heavy gold signet ring. "What do they say about great minds thinking alike?"

"Just that, I guess," Emma smiled as he slipped the ring onto his little finger. "We're not quite conventional yet, but we seem to be moving in that direction."

"We'll *never* be conventional, Emma mine," he pronounced. "You, at least, are far too extraordinary."

"Well, since *you* are extra special," she grinned, wrapping her arms around his neck, "we'll just settle for what we are."

13

EMMA LAY STILL, gazing wide-eyed into the darkness as she had done for the last ten minutes. The only sounds in the room were the ticking of the clock—suddenly very loud—and Mark's deep, even breathing. He was a very quiet, still sleeper. When he got out of bed in the morning, the sheets on his side of the bed were hardly rumpled. This strange, disconnected thought came and went as she finally acknowledged that she was experiencing the symptoms of labor.

"Mark?" She spoke his name softly, knowing that he

would wake instantly.

"What is it, sweet?" He sounded wide awake and alert, as he always did. He could move from deep sleep into instant wakefulness without any of the intervening drowsiness that kept her grumbling and grumping for about twenty minutes after she woke up. Unless, of course, Mark took matters into his own hands, as he usually did—another disconnected thought.

"Things seem to be happening rather rapidly," she stated calmly.

Mark switched on a lamp, bathing the room in a soft, muted glow. Then he reached for his watch, laid a very gentle, featherlike hand on her stomach, frowning at the second hand as he timed the contraction and the very short interval between it and its successor.

"Someone's in a hurry," he said matter-of-factly, his calmness matching her own. "How long has it been going on?"

"Only a few minutes," she murmured and then stopped, concentrated on breathing her way through the next contraction. "I woke up very suddenly," she finished with a slight gasp.

"I should think you did!" He smiled at her, pulling back the covers. "Let's see just how long we've got."

It was most extraordinary, Emma reflected absently; she wasn't at all worried about anything, and Mark was certainly not giving her any reason to be anxious.

"You're fully dilated, sweet," he said coolly. "I can feel the head. Looks as if we're on our own with this one."

"Can you remember how to do it?" She managed a somewhat weak, distracted smile.

"I haven't delivered a baby since I was in med school," he said cheerfully, "but I'm assuming it's like riding a bicycle—one of those tricks you never forget!" He picked up the bedside phone. "I think we'll get Meg up here, though, and at least this household has an unusually well-equipped medical kit."

Emma's body suddenly behaved in the most extraordinary fashion, curving with an irresistible pushing sensation. "Wow!" she breathed in a certain amount of awe. "This infant is not about to wait for anyone!"

"Are you all right, sweet?" After summoning Meg, Mark had dropped to his knees at the foot of the bed. "We've got most things in the kit, but nothing as sophisticated as anesthetic."

"Don't need it," she gasped. "This isn't painful; it's just plain hard labor!"

"You are an amazing woman." He chuckled. "Bear down again—that's my girl! You're doing beautifully."

Meg exploded into the room, wide-eyed and disheveled, clutching the leather medical kit.

"Lord!" she exclaimed, taking in the scene. "Don't you two ever do anything like anyone else?"

"There are three of us involved in this one." Emma managed an abstracted smile.

"Stop lollygagging, both of you," Mark commanded. "You're distracting me!" Laughter, and something else, lurked in his voice, but Emma didn't have time to identify it. She was far too busy.

"What should I do?" Meg asked.

"Get a mirror," Emma demanded. "I want to see it happen."

"Better hurry, then," Mark said calmly. "Don't push again, Emma. The head's about to crown."

Emma struggled into a half-sitting position as Meg piled pillows behind her shoulders, and watched fascinated in the mirror as the sleek, round head emerged from her body.

"There we go, little one." Mark was talking to the baby now, his voice soft and cajoling. "Let's turn your shoulders just a tiny bit, that's it, and we'll have you out in this big, wide world in no time."

Hot tears of joy spilled from Emma's eyes as she listened to his gentle voice, felt the sudden slither as this newborn person found safety in Mark's large, competent, waiting hands.

"Let's have a big yell, now, small one," Mark urged, his little finger deftly removing the mucus from the tiny mouth. A loud, shrill, complaining wail rang through the room.

"Such an importunate little daughter we have, Emma mine." His own eyes shone with tears as he looked at her in this moment of complete togetherness. Her smile reached for his as she tried to encompass him with her loving, joyful gaze.

"Give her to me," she whispered, holding out her arms.

Mark laid the tiny scrap of humanity on her stomach, and Emma reached down to hold their daughter as he cut and tied the cord, before wrapping the baby in a blanket Meg passed to him and putting the child against her mother's breast.

"She's got a lot of curly hair." Emma laughed softly. "Just like yours when you get out of the shower. Isn't she absolutely beautiful?"

"Absolutely." He smiled. "Just like her mother." His lips brushed her damp forehead, and his hand raked through the limp, sweat-soaked strands of her hair. "Give her to Meg for a minute, sweet. You're not quite through yet."

Reluctantly, she handed the tiny bundle into Meg's eager arms, felt Mark's hand, warm on her abdomen, pushing down with a firm, cupped palm, heard his quiet instruction, "Once more, my love."

She delivered the placenta with one final effort and sat back again, reaching for the baby, cradling her against her breast, touching the tiny button of her nose with the tip of a finger.

"Meg, you're crying!" she accused, wiping her own eyes with the back of her free hand.

"What a wonderful way to be born!" Meg exclaimed, sniffing vigorously as the tears spilled down her cheeks. "I can't help it. I'm sorry, Em."

"Somebody better get the tissues." Mark gave a watery chuckle. "Otherwise, we're all going to drown!" He blew his nose fiercely, and then was all brisk decision. "Everything looks fine to me. I'll call the ambulance now. It's time you two were tucked in, my sweet Emma."

"No!" she exclaimed energetically, clutching the baby to her. "Beth and I are going nowhere right now!"

Mark regarded her thoughtfully, a slight smile glinting in his eyes. "No?" he questioned.

"No," Emma reiterated stoutly. "We've already done the hard part. I see no reason why we should be traumatized by that January wind, just in order to be absorbed into a hospital system that, at this point, we don't need."

Mark scratched his head, wanted to laugh, and eventually

did so, uproariously. Nothing would change his Emma! "You are an impossible woman, Emma Grantham!" he said stoutly. "You really won't go?"

"Won't," she said firmly, but her eyes said, "Will, if it'll make you more comfortable."

He thought for a minute and then shook his head resignedly. "I can't think of one single medical reason why you should, but I'm neither a gynecologist nor a pediatrician."

"Neil and Patrick will make house calls in the morning, won't they?" Emma asked softly. "I don't want to go anywhere tonight, Mark."

He heard the plea, read the message in her eyes, realized that if he insisted she would go without complaint, and knew that he couldn't insist.

"There's a case of Veuve Clicquot in the cellar," he said, grinning. "I'm sure we can reward old friends who come to visit."

"I think I'll make some tea." Meg moved toward the door, smiling broadly. "It's usual on these occasions."

"I can't think of anything I'd like more right now," Emma announced, "except for a bath."

"You first and then Beth," Mark said cheerfully, rolling up the sleeves of his robe and disappearing into the bathroom.

It was quite some time later when Beth Forrest—bathed, diapered, and dressed—was tucked into her crib in the corner of the room, snuffling plaintively and randomly as she adapted to her strange new environment.

Emma, feeling fresh and clean herself, curled into the new, sweet-smelling sheets with a sigh of peace and contentment. Meg had returned to her own bed with eyes still moist.

Emma regarded Mark through half-closed eyes as he stood looking into the crib where he had just deposited his daughter, an expression of total wonderment on his face.

"I'm cold," she muttered. Instantly, he turned and came over to the bed, throwing off his robe.

"Can't have that, Emma mine, wife of mine, now, can we?" He slipped between the sheets, and she snuggled against his warm strength.

"You certainly haven't forgotten how to ride a bicycle, husband."

"When someone else is providing the training wheels, it's very simple." He laughed.

Her laughter joined his, and then, through a drowsy haze, Emma murmured, "We've had a rough time this last year, my love."

"A rough spot or two," he corrected, smoothing her hair in the darkness. "But we've learned a lot, sweet."

"What have you learned?" She crept even closer to him.

"That you are all and everything to me—that you bound my life and fill it." His arms clutched her tightly. "And you, Emma mine, what have you learned?"

"That I am Emma yours and you are Mark mine."

"And Sam and Beth?" His arms tightened.

"Will grow and flourish, as we shall."

Center Point Publishing
600 Brooks Road • PO Box 1
Thorndike ME 04986-0001 USA

(207) 568-3717

US & Canada:
1 800 929-9108